Spells of Summer

Publication Date: September 10, 2018

AQUARIOTS
UNLIMITED

ISBN-13: 978-1-7750252-7-6

Contents

The Best Laid Plan

Chapter 1

Emmilene gazed across the road at him with longing eyes. He was ruggedly handsome, with a muscular physique that showed itself even beneath his layers and overcoat, which were worn with a casual disregard. His light brown, almost ginger hair was thick and upswept at the ends, and his scruffy triangular beard had longer tufts at the corners of his jawline. He didn't have the same concern for decorous grooming as did other gentlemen, which made for a rather untamed, but undeniably attractive, appearance. His name was Roderick Ruttledge, and he was the most affluent bachelor in the city. But money didn't matter to Emmilene. All she wanted was the chance to love him in person.

She'd seen him around town many times before, and each glimpse was a delight. Everyone knew who he was on sight. He often had some young lady or other on his arm – showing her around and taking her to lavish events. Emmilene wished she could be one of those girls, just so she could spend time with him.

Roderick came here to the inn every day at noon, to chat with the newspaper man at his stall before giving him a fivepence tip and going inside for lunch. After noticing Roderick at that spot one time, Emmilene started returning daily to watch him for the ten minutes he spent there. But she stayed on the far side of the street; it would be improper for a woman to approach a man. And without being introduced, at that. Not that her family could have done so for her, since they weren't wealthy or prestigious enough to be socializing with a man of his class. However, if Roderick was the one to choose her, that was another matter. So Emmilene waited, and hoped one day he would look her way.

***

Roderick stood speaking with the newsvendor. After the man finished what he was saying, he looked across the street at a young woman in a pastel-green dress. "You know, that poor girl's been pining after you for the longest time."

Roderick turned his eyes to her with appraising interest. "Really?" He hadn't noticed her before. She *was* quite comely, with a wavy mass of golden-brown hair, and a pleasing figure; still slim, but with all the right curves.

"Comes here every day, same time as you, like clockwork. Just to stare at you with those doe eyes."

If she already fancied herself infatuated with him, that would make it all the easier to get her into bed. Roderick toyed with the idea for a moment, then decided to humour her. He was going to make her day.

***

As Emmilene watched, Roderick

began to cross the street to her. Her breath caught, hope leaping within her. *Can it be?* His gaze was definitely on her. He came right up to her, and it was almost surreal. She'd never been this close to him before.

"I hear you've been admiring me," Roderick purred, slowly lifting her hand to give it a kiss, meeting her eyes all the while. "Let me return the favour."

She stared at him with big eyes, and dipped a brief curtsy. "You are too kind, Mr. Ruttledge," she murmured breathlessly.

He showed a slight smile, eyes glittering. "Call me Roderick," he invited instead. Emmilene's heart was beating fast. "What might your name be?"

"Emmilene. Emmilene Hetherley." Her wish was finally coming to pass! He was actually speaking with her!

"A name well suited to your beauty.

Tell me, Miss Emmilene...have you yet been to see the new clocktower?" He offered his arm.

She could hardly believe he wanted to accompany her somewhere. She tentatively set her hand in the crook of his arm, and couldn't help noticing how muscular it felt, even through the coatsleeve.

They turned to start strolling along together, and Roderick continued to coax comments out of her with leading remarks of his own.

Over an hour later, after they'd toured the outside of the tower, he kissed her hand again and invited her to join him on the morrow at the tea shop. Emmilene could hardly contain her excitement as she agreed. As soon as Roderick had gone on by, she set a hand over her heart in an attempt to calm herself. *He wants to see me again!*

Roderick came to meet her every day, and they spent progressively longer amounts of time together. He flirted and teased and charmed and romanced, making clear his intention to woo her. He escorted her to banquets where they sampled fine cuisine; to ballrooms where they danced hand-in-hand; to plays of a dramatic romantic nature that often made her gasp and set a hand on his arm; and to boutiques where he bought her anything she fancied, no matter how pricy. Emmilene found it all very glamorous, but what she cherished most was just being in his company, all the talk they shared; what she thought and felt, their lives and interests, or just pleasant repartee for the enjoyment of it.

Roderick took every opportunity to get closer to her; helping her down from carriages, guiding her with a hand on her back, letting her use his arm as a brace as she stepped over puddles. Though they'd only known each other for a few weeks, Emmilene didn't mind; she could imagine every touch was an indication of his affection for her. He gave her gifts of jewelry and perfumes, and murmured sweet sentiments in her ear. He made her feel so treasured. She was sure it meant he was starting to care for her as much as she did for him.

One night, he took her to the biggest ball of the season, held in the grand hall, where every local notable personage would be in attendance. Emmilene wore her best new gown of navy blue satin, along with white elbow-length gloves. Roderick held her close as they danced for hours, sweeping across the floor amidst a heady blur of enveloping music and other couples. It seemed at once to last for a dreamlike lifetime and to be over too soon. When she and Roderick finally left and proceeded down the wide stone steps, she was still rosy-cheeked from the activity, rhapsodizing to him about the experience as they walked across the square.

She was in too much of a whirl of exhilaration to realize he'd backed her into a corner. She only broke off from her breathless enthusing when she glanced up to see him watching her with an intense gaze. Before she could react, he slid his gloved hand onto the side of her face, and leaned in to give her an ardent kiss.

Her heart leapt with surprised delight. The feel of his ginger stubble brushing her skin, the feel of his moist lips on hers, touched her so tenderly, so deeply, that she was filled with affectionate adoration for him. Oh, it was just what she'd always wanted!

His other hand was resting on her waist, and she set her own on his arm. Emmilene knew it was scandalous for an unmarried couple to kiss, but at this point she didn't care – and it bespoke of further intentions he must have for their future.

When at last he pulled away, it left her heart racing and her body atingle with warmth. Roderick met her gaze from a few inches away, dark eyes twinkling.

Emmilene glanced down demurely, then lifted her eyes to his again, harbouring a small smile.

It was then that she knew she was in love with him.

From then on, they became even closer, touching more often and stealing occasional kisses where no one would see.

One summer afternoon, they were strolling down the sidewalk with Emmilene's arms wrapped around his. Watching her, Roderick leaned a bit closer. "It's sweltering out here, isn't it," he purred. "It's only a block to my apartment suite. Shall we head inside?"

Emmilene studied him. It was inadvisable for a young woman to be alone with a man in his own residence. But she trusted Roderick. She nodded.

He showed her into his building, and they went up to his rooms on the third floor. He got the door for her, then followed her in. With his hands on the knob behind him, he leaned back on the door to quietly close it, watching her with lowered brows while she drifted in to the middle of the drawing room.

It was a luxurious place, furnished with upholstered seats and varnished tables that still contributed a sense of masculine independence. The russet wallpaper made the room look even warmer than it already was with the summer sunlight coming in.

Roderick crossed to the window, and lowered the sash. He turned back to Emmilene, meeting her eyes with a simmering gaze. The still air was thick with allure. Roderick came slowly over to her, until he stood very close. "Emmilene...I must profess what I feel for you."

Her heartbeat quickened with expectant joy. Could it be that Roderick loved her too?

"Every day I've spent with you has made it grow stronger." He rested his hand on her waist. "I can't keep resisting it. I know you feel it too." Roderick inched his face beside hers, and the proximity made warmth rise in her cheeks. And...elsewhere.

"All your wildest fantasies..." Roderick murmured by her ear, his breath warm on her neck. "All the things you've never felt..." He stroked the backs of his fingers over her shoulder. "All the intimacy you desire..." He drew her hips closer with his other hand, and Emmilene felt a surge of yearning. "I can give it to you."

Her breathing became shaky.

Roderick turned his head, his lips hovering near her cheek. "Will you let me?"

Emmilene shuddered with temptation. "Yes," she breathed.

He stooped and kissed her, more deeply and lingeringly than ever before. The feel of him inside her mouth made her loins kindle with juicy stirrings. His burst of passion was overwhelming, and it left her rather breathless.

His presence was so magnetic, his untucked shirt so enticing, Emmilene couldn't withhold the urge to explore him.

She slid her hands up under his shirt, feeling the firm muscles of his bare torso. Roderick spared her the trouble and pulled his shirt off over his head, tossing it heedlessly to the floor. Then he sank his hands in her mass of hair, holding her face between both of them as he engaged her mouth with his again.

Roderick advanced so she had to step backwards along with him. He backed her up against the wall rather firmly, cornering her there with his sinewy arms on either side of her. Emmilene was quivering all over, but it was from anticipation. The moment she'd long been dreaming of was about to happen! She loved him so much, she gave nary a thought to expressing it before their wedding. She looped her arms onto his shoulders, and laced her fingers behind his neck. Roderick pressed his body against hers, so very warm, and...masculine.

He hoisted her legs up onto his hips, so her draping skirt concealed everything below their waists. With her head now slightly above his, Roderick pinned her against the wall.

As they resumed kissing, Emmilene curled her fingers into the longer tufts of his ginger side-whiskers, clutching them between her knuckles. The tingles he made her body feel were as hot as ginger, too.

Chapter 2

In the days that followed, Emmilene all too aware that Roderick didn't come to visit her. When she received no word from him either, she went to the same place she had first met him. He arrived there on time, as always. He saw her too, she was sure of it; their eyes met briefly across the distance. But he didn't come over to her, didn't even acknowledge her with a wave, nod, or smile – he just went about his business like she wasn't there. Maybe he was just otherwise occupied, and would call on her when he could. Emmilene returned every day to wait for him, just as she had before – but Roderick never crossed to her, even as the days turned into weeks. She didn't understand it. She just hoped that, in time, he would come back to her.

One afternoon, she kept gazing after him even after he had gone inside the inn. At least this way, she got to see him for a little while each day.

A carriage came barrelling up the puddle-ridden street, and she jumped back on the sidewalk to avoid the splash. She bumped into the chest of someone, who set steadying hands on her shoulders. Surprised, Emmilene tilted her head back to look up at the tanned, almost olive-skinned face above her, which belonged to a tall, dark-haired young lieutenant in a drab-green uniform. "Oh." Emmilene chuckled sheepishly, hastily sidestepping out of his way and turning to face him. "Pardon me."

His expression was accommodating, though, and faintly amused. "It's quite all right," he reassured. Then his face became curious. "What's a young lady like yourself doing waiting out here on a corner? I've seen you at this same spot a few times."

Emmilene lowered her eyes, then looked out across the street again. "I just come here to get a glimpse of the man who used to court me."

The lieutenant's brow furrowed. "He

doesn't call on you anymore?"

"We haven't met in weeks." She sighed. "I'm sure Roderick will find the time soon."

"Roderick?" the lieutenant repeated. "That wouldn't perchance be Roderick Ruttledge? I know him!"

She turned to the man in delight. "You do?"

"He and I have been friends since we were boys. I'm Ishwar Langhorne."

She offered her hand in introduction. "Emmilene Hetherley."

He paused in taking her hand. "You're *that* Emmilene?" he remarked. "He's told me all about you."

Her heart lifted. "He speaks of me? Will you talk with me about him?"

Ishwar's expression sobered a little, and he gestured toward the sidewalk. "Shall we go for a stroll?" Emmilene took the arm he offered, and they turned to start walking.

They talked about Roderick for hours, Ishwar sharing stories of their childhood. Emmilene and the lieutenant met again over the next few days, and they soon became well acquainted.

When they came to a teahouse, Ishwar sat down with her on a bench outside it. The lieutenant's face was earnest. "I know you only want to hear the best of Roderick, but you must know why he hasn't been seeing you anymore." He waited, but she didn't respond. "That man is a rake, Emmilene," he imparted to her, solemn and regretful. "He doesn't care for you, and he never did. All you ever were to him was a pretty skirt to chase."

She was silent for a moment. "You don't speak of him as a friend," she observed instead.

Ishwar showed a wry smile. "I've known for years what kind of man he is; it takes a certain lenience to be his friend anyway. I'm saying it outright so that you too will understand his nature for what it is."

"I already knew he was partial to dalliance," Emmilene said quietly. "But what we had was more than that. I know he'll come to see that, too."

"I admire your loyalty," Ishwar remarked, with genuine surprise. "But I doubt it'll make any difference to him. He's done this before; charmed a lady until he got what he wanted from her, then left her in the lurch." He lowered his voice, watching her gently. "He boasted to me of his conquest of you. I know the two of you were intimate together."

Her cheeks grew hot to hear it spoken of by another – but just as much of it was from remembering the pleasure of her time with Roderick. "I have no regrets."

"I think you need to fully consider what he's done to you. Once they find out you've already been with a man, no one will want to marry you."

Emmilene looked up with some concern. But she was more resigned than devastated.

"No one, that is, except me. I'd be willing to overlook that and be a husband to you anyway. I could provide you with a secure future, and a respectable standing."

She almost considered that for a moment. Then she dropped her eyes. "That's very kind of you," she murmured. "But it won't be necessary."

Ishwar inclined his head. "Very well," he replied. "But I suggest that you at least stop waiting for him every day. If it hasn't garnered his attention after two weeks, it's not going to. Your time would be better spent starting to move on."

Emmilene looked down the street, toward the inn. "I will always wait for him."

And so she did. But every time, after Roderick just went on his way again, Ishwar came around to keep her company. He even insisted on taking her to events so she wouldn't miss out, and also brought her to meet his parents and his sister Indira, who took to Emmilene like a sister herself.

***

Roderick saw Emmilene across the road several times without giving her a second thought. But after a while, he found himself thinking of her on occasion, even while going about his day. It was just a snippet here and there; a memory of her inviting green eyes, the floral scent of her perfume, the way her warm, soft body felt on his. And once it came to him, he ended up dwelling on it longer. No other girl had lingered in his mind so. He began to feel something – a yearning – that could even be called nostalgia. He wanted to have her again. Maybe he shouldn't have been so hasty to leave her. Perhaps, with her especial willingness, he could have gotten a few more times out of her before she began expecting a commitment. Maybe he still could, if she was patient enough to be waiting for him every day.

Roderick walked up the street one day, and spotted Emmilene on the other side. She hadn't noticed him yet. He regarded her for a moment, pausing, then decided to go up to her. He crossed the road, weaving between the other people pushing handcarts or leading donkeys. Then he started up the sidewalk toward her, passing by a window display of a dress shop. As he neared where the jutting building formed a nook, he slowed, stopping to look at Emmilene past the corner. She was still gazing across at the inn he usually frequented.

But he found himself faced with a most unfamiliar hesitation. He'd never gone back to a girl after he'd had his way with her. And Roderick Ruttledge wasn't the one to supplicate women. They were the ones who lined up for a chance to be with him. What was he to even say to explain his absence? It had been weeks already; Emmilene probably didn't want anything to do with him anymore. He would just be setting himself up for rejection. If it had been anyone else, it wouldn't have mattered to him.

Then a young woman joined

Emmilene, who turned to her to give her a hug of glad welcome.

Roderick's heart sank a little in resignation. He'd missed his chance. He couldn't speak with her now, when she had company. Besides, it looked like she was moving on with her life; just there to meet a friend, not gaze across the road at him anymore.

Slowly, he backed away from the corner, then turned and walked away.

Chapter 3

Roderick sat sprawled in a chair with one arm on his desk, his back to the large windows of his apartment study. He stared at the glass of gin in his hand, then downed another swallow of it. He felt numb inside, and not just from the liquor.

Emmilene was still on his mind. Why hadn't he gone up to her? He'd never lost his gumption like that before. He had always been the master of confidence.

The door opened, and Ishwar strolled in without knocking. He was all neat and proper in his olive-drab uniform, in contrast to Roderick's untucked shirt and unbuttoned coat.

Roderick eyed him expressionlessly. He wasn't in the mood for company right now.

"You look miserable," Ishwar remarked cheerfully. "Care to air your woes to a sympathetic ear?"

Roderick swirled the gin in his glass. "Not – in – the slightest," he articulated crisply. He took another drink.

"Well, then, I'll just carry on with

what I came here to say," Ishwar went on briskly, and pulled up a chair. "Remember your latest conquest, Emmilene?"

Roderick glanced up, attention piqued at the echo of his thoughts.

"I've met her; she's quite a lovely thing. She and I are courting now, as it happens."

Roderick watched him flatly. Was Ishwar trying to make him jealous? It wouldn't work; Roderick never got emotionally attached to any of his flings. After he was done with them, he couldn't care less who got involved with them next.

"We've laid together, quite a few times." Ishwar grew a smirk. "You're right, she is quite the passionflower in bed."

Roderick's gaze hardened. He was beginning to feel a stir of resentment in spite of himself. To hear the lieutenant talk about

Emmilene that way, so insolently...to imagine Ishwar defiling her, the same woman Roderick had been with first...it *did* make him seethe. No one had ever flaunted their appropriation of his erstwhile lover.

"But even when we're making love, all she can talk about is you. She kept comparing it to her time with you, and she says you were better." Ishwar paused to study him. "She must still be deeply in love with you. Even after I told her all about your previous exploits, she didn't change her mind about you. That's some kind of dedication." His expression became stern. "It was wrong of you to toy with her affections," he chided. "A good woman like her doesn't deserve that."

Roderick felt a twinge, and dropped his eyes. He felt bad about hurting her. Was this...guilt?

"And based on your most

uncharacteristic melancholy, I'd say you care for her just as much."

Roderick flicked his eyes up to Ishwar in surprise.

"Consider it, now. Can you honestly say you don't?"

Roderick's absent gaze drifted aside. Whenever he thought of Emmilene, he envisioned her waves of golden-brown hair, her radiant smile...the spark they'd had together. He wanted that again. And without her now, he felt empty. He'd never experienced these emotions for anyone else before. Could it be love?

Roderick sighed. "What do you suggest I do?"

"Marry her," Ishwar stated simply, and Roderick glanced up at him. "I know such a thought has never crossed your mind before, but you won't find another woman as devoted as she is. It's the decent thing to do, and you're the only one she'll be happy with. If you care about her at all, you'll want that for her."

And Ishwar left him to contemplate that. Roderick tried to find if there was any reason he shouldn't marry her. Her family was much less wealthy than his. But he had no need to marry for money. There certainly wasn't anyone else he could think of that he'd rather spend a lifetime with. He shuddered at the thought. Most of the other girls he'd dallied with were insufferably featherbrained, or had irritating mannerisms, or weren't all that pretty to begin with. He hadn't even liked them. He'd only been in it for the conquest, whether or not they were pleasant company.

Emmilene, though...she was refined, yet wholesome; intelligent, but gentle. There wasn't a single thing about her that was disagreeable. Roderick could imagine her making the ideal wife; docile and patient and willing. And then he wouldn't have to look further than his own wife for gratification.

Of course, then he couldn't enjoy the thrill of pursuing new women, either. But at a certain point, the turnaround time between scores became tiresome anyway. And much as he hated to admit it, there might eventually come a time – many decades from now – when he might not be able to attract the eyes of young ladies quite the same. If he married now, he wouldn't have to worry about that, even if that meant not taking advantage of all those perfectly good years of eligibility. Besides, there was no guarantee that anyone he found from now on would be any better a catch than Emmilene.

The next evening, Roderick walked to

the Hetherley townhouse on the southeast side of town. He went up the stone steps, and paused before using the brass doorknocker. He wasn't used to taking the polite approach, but he was in a position of supplication this time, so it wouldn't do to barge in uninvited.

The door was opened by the doorman, and Roderick told him he'd come to see Emmilene. The man let Roderick in and closed the door behind him.

"Mr. Ruttledge has come calling," the doorman announced, then withdrew into another room.

Emmilene drifted into the foyer, and hopeful warmth lit in her eyes when she saw him. "Roderick," she murmured.

Her reception was encouraging. He stepped a bit closer. "I know it's been too long. But I'm here now. You've been on my mind ever since, like no one else ever has.

What I mean to say is..." He took her hands in his. "I...I've come to have a deep and indelible love for you."

Her breath caught. "Oh, Roderick!" she breathed, and wrapped her arms about his neck in a hug.

He drew Emmilene close to him, his heart filling with a most affectionate and poignant sensation, stronger than even he would have expected. It felt so good to hold her. Her body fit so perfectly against his own. Her sweet nature, that he was now so fond of, emanated from every soft, warm contour of her figure.

Roderick backed up a little to meet her eyes. "There's something I must ask you," he went on. "I don't even know how to pose it, for I've never asked it before, nor even considered it." He lifted her hand in both of his. "Will you be my wife?"

Eyes big and glistening, Emmilene set her fingertips to her mouth for a moment, partially covering a quivering smile. "I've been waiting months to say yes to that," she whispered.

Breaking into a lopsided grin, Roderick set his hands on either side of her face and leaned in to kiss her. Her moist, full lips were just as luscious as he remembered, the spark they kindled within him just as strong. Emmilene set her hands on his chest, and willingly reciprocated. His desire simmered to life again, spurred by how attracted he was to her. He lingered on her round lower lip, then gave her another kiss. He didn't want to stop kissing her, but he reluctantly restrained himself; this was neither the time nor the place for what he wanted to do. He stayed with his forehead bowed against hers, their warm breaths a bit unsteady on each other's faces.

"Shall we sit?" Emmilene suggested. She pulled back, and they adjourned into the parlour, settling onto a settee. She leaned closer to him, resting her shoulder on his chest.

"I suppose you know you're not the only woman I've laid with." Roderick fixed his stony gaze on the floor. "I don't blame you for doing the same with Ishwar."

Emmilene drew back abruptly, looking at him with a scandalized frown. "What? I never sought those comforts from him. We only ever conversed as friends."

He stared at her. Then he realized. Ishwar must have just told him that to get him riled up. Roderick was on the verge of becoming indignant, but then had to admit that it had worked. It was a good thing, too; it was what it had taken to get him to go back to her. He studied Emmilene with wondering admiration. "Your loyalty is unequalled." He'd done nothing to earn it.

Her eyes drifted shyly down to his hand where it rested on his knee, and she entwined her fingers with his. "You're the only one I've ever wanted," she said softly. She set her head on his shoulder. "Now we can give our families the good news."

Roderick wasn't looking forward to that. His parents were sure to frown upon it, since they would consider Emmilene beneath his station. But he supposed it had to be done. They'd done enough sneaking around. She deserved to at least have her wedding be a public occasion.

Chapter 4

On the morrow, Roderick went to the Ruttledge estate, situated some distance outside the south end of town. A long, winding gravel laneway ended in a circle before the front steps. It was an impressive mansion of sandstone and dark grey slate roofs, with plenty of rock garden landscaping.

Roderick informed his parents that he intended to host a dinner at the manor. Then he had invitation notes delivered to Emmilene's family, and to the Langhornes as well, to show Ishwar that Roderick had taken his advice to heart.

After dark, the Hetherleys arrived first in a carriage, followed by Ishwar and his parents. As they disembarked, Roderick went out to accompany Emmilene, and the butler saw the rest of them in.

They all met in the dining hall. Roderick and Emmilene sat beside each other, while her parents were given the seats of honour at the head of the long table. Everyone exchanged the usual pleasantries, but none of them appeared as if they knew what they were gathered for – all looking from one to the other for clues. Mrs. Ruttledge, with her blonde hair up in a tight bun that accentuated her sharp features, was eyeing the plump and almost folksy Mrs. Hetherley with disdain. Red-haired Mr. Ruttledge idly ran the back of a thumbnail over one of his mutton-chop sideburns as he regarded Mr. Langhorne. After the glasses of wine had been served, but before the food arrived, Roderick spoke up.

"The reason I've invited you all here is to make an announcement." Roderick studied each of their faces. "Emmilene and I are engaged to be married."

There was a floored silence.

"Married? To *her*?" Mrs. Ruttledge repeated. "Why, she's little more than a commoner."

"Come now, Roderick," Mr. Ruttledge scoffed. "We all know you're not the type to settle down."

Roderick compressed his lips with flat determination. "I assure you, I have every intention of marrying her."

Mrs. Hetherley had her hand to her mouth, looking from Ishwar to Emmilene and back. "Oh, dear, this is a dreadful mistake," she murmured.

Roderick bristled. "Make no mistake, this is just as much Emmilene's decision as it is mine."

"You don't understand – this arrangement is simply not possible," Mr. Langhorne put in. "For the simple fact that she is already betrothed to our son."

Roderick stared at the man, speechless. Then he looked at Ishwar. The lieutenant wore a rather smug look. *What...?* Then Roderick set his jaw, and stood up so his chair scraped back over the floor. "I don't know what you're playing at, but this farce changes nothing," he growled. He took Emmilene's hand, and she rose, too. "Emmilene and I will be wed, with or without your approval."

With that, he turned and stormed out with her. After a pause, the room behind him erupted into commotion. From the sound of it, they were just getting in each other's way.

Then footsteps followed them, and Roderick looked over his shoulder to see Ishwar sauntering out from the archway.

"Wait outside," he muttered to Emmilene without looking back at her. After she was out the door, Roderick advanced on Ishwar.

"What is the meaning of this?" he demanded. "I thought you told me to marry her!"

"Indeed I did," Ishwar admitted

calmly, with a trace of a smirk. "But I didn't say I'd make it easy for you."

Roderick stared at him for a consternated moment. "How do you know I won't just give her up?"

"Because I know you," he replied simply, but grimly. "You want what you can't have, and you'd never back down from a competition."

Roderick narrowed his eyes. "And I never lose one, either."

Before anyone else could come after them, he spun and strode outside, where Emmilene stood on the porch. Without slowing, he gripped her hand, his fingers linked with hers. As they swiftly descended the stone steps, he looked over at her. "Did you know about this?" It came out a little harsher than he'd intended; he was still fuming at Ishwar.

"No," she murmured sadly, eyes downcast. "I never accepted any proposal. Our parents must have arranged it when they saw that we were spending time together."

She was such a gentle soul. She still thought the best of those who were plotting against them.

They climbed into the waiting carriage, and at Roderick's signal, the driver slapped the reins to set them racing off for the city.

Behind them, Emmilene's parents came rushing out onto the porch and stopped short. "Come back here with our daughter!" Mr. Hetherley called after them. "You have no claim on her!"

Once the Ruttledge house was out of sight, Roderick faced forward again. But his gaze was downturned in frowning thought.

"I can't take you back to your parents'

residence," he said, and Emmilene looked up. "They'd just keep you there, to keep us apart, and force you to marry Ishwar."

Her eyes held concern. "Should we stay at your suite?" she suggested in a small voice.

Roderick met her eyes, tempted by the thought of repeating what they had done the last time they were there. But then he dropped his gaze. "No. That's the first place they'd look," he muttered. He started thinking again, then came up with an alternative. "I'll put you up at a first-rate boardinghouse. Then we'll pick out a bridal dress for you tomorrow. That'll show them we're in earnest."

Roderick leaned over Emmilene's seat and slid the panel open to tell the driver to take them to the new destination on the northwest side of town.

When they got there, Roderick paid for a room on the third floor. He went up with Emmilene and opened the door for her, then followed her in and closed it behind him.

He went to the window, and parted the curtain to peer out at the dark street below, looking up and down it. No one seemed to have followed them there.

He turned back to the room. Emmilene had seated herself on the foot of the bed, and was watching him with upturned eyes. She looked so demure and feminine, with her hands folded in her lap. Roderick became aware of what she must be thinking, with the intimate setting, the quiet depths of the night, just the two of them alone together, finally. He could so easily push her down on the bed...

With an effort, he reined in his desires. "I'll go have the kitchen prepare something for us." They'd left the manor before supper had been served, after all. It was more important that Emmilene not miss a meal.

Roderick went down and brought back a platter of bread and stew-filled bowls himself, so there would be all the less people to see Emmilene and potentially disclose her location. After handing her the tray, he ate his share in a chair by the window as he kept watch.

By the time he was done, Emmilene was sound asleep on the bed, her arms curled up before her. Roderick couldn't help a slight smile of wry fondness. There would be no fooling around tonight. It was only fun if they were awake, anyway. But a touch of tenderness also rose in him. He got up to take a knitted throw from one of the chaises, and settled it over Emmilene. Then he returned to his post to look out into the night.

When morning came, Roderick took her to the dress shop to pick out a wedding gown. Entering the sunny store, they started browsing the racks and wicker figures displaying dresses of both white and all colours.

"Buy whichever dress your heart desires," Roderick told her softly. "Money is no object."

Emmilene looked them over, setting a hand on one to feel the fabric or taking another off the rack to see it full-length.

Behind them, the shop door banged open. "Ruttledge!" a stern voice barked. Roderick turned to see Mr. Langhorne, Ishwar, and Emmilene's father starting toward them, weaving between the dress racks.

Roderick spun and towed Emmilene along by the hand as they dashed for the back door.

The men chased after them, and Roderick dodged out of sight down a side street. But then he spotted Ishwar at the alley mouth trying to head them off, so Roderick had to pull Emmilene into another shop to run out through a side door.

Over the next few hours, there were several more near-misses as the others pursued them through town, but Roderick and Emmilene managed to elude them. After things finally quieted down, Roderick arranged for a carriage to meet them on an empty street. He helped Emmilene into it and closed the door for her.

"Going somewhere?"

Roderick turned to see Ishwar strolling up the street toward them.

"Absconding with a young woman? You should know better."

Roderick took a few strides toward him. "Give up this charade! She never agreed to marry you."

"Either way, she belongs at home until the wedding."

Hooves clattered on cobblestones behind Roderick, and he whirled as the carriage charged away. Emmilene leaned out the window, looking back at him with sorrow in her eyes.

"That'll be her parents now," Ishwar mused.

Roderick glared at him, but the lieutenant was already ducking down a side alley. Ishwar must have planned the whole thing. He always seemed to be one step ahead. Roderick watched the distant carriage, and beat a fist on his thigh, cursing himself for letting it happen. There'd be no point going to the Hetherley townhouse; in all likelihood, they wouldn't even let him in to see her. He was going to have to think of some other way to settle this once and for all.

Chapter 5

Roderick entered the bank to make a withdrawal, but to his disbelief the banker refused his transaction request. When Roderick insisted on knowing why, he was told he no longer had authority to access the account. Roderick turned on his heel and left, heading to the Ruttledge estate to see what this was all about.

On his way through town to find a cheap cabriolet, he noticed people looking at him and shaking their heads in disapproval, muttering amongst themselves. He caught a few snatches of "cad" and "disgrace". He began to feel a creeping apprehension. What rumour was going around about him now?

When he got to the manor, the butler opened the door only a little, and seemed reluctant when Roderick told him to inform the Ruttledges of his arrival. But Roderick pushed past him when he saw his parents in the dim foyer beyond.

"The bank has locked me out. Would you know anything about that?" Roderick demanded of them.

Mr. Ruttledge had his brows drawn

down. "It was our doing. We know all about your many *indiscretions* with women," he hissed.

Roderick stopped short, aghast. How had they found out...?

Mrs. Ruttledge shook her head slowly. "How could you, Roderick?" she whispered.

Mr. Ruttledge's face was stern. "You are a disgrace to this family's name. You are hereby disentitled from all access to our estate."

Roderick stared at him, dread sinking into the pit of his stomach. Then it gave rise to indignation. "You can't disown me! I'm your only heir!"

"We *have* no heir."

Roderick clenched his jaw, then jabbed a finger at them, eyes narrowed. "Don't pretend you didn't know about it all along. You just turned a blind eye to spare your own reputation."

Mr. Ruttledge jerked a nod at the butler, who took Roderick's arm to escort him off the premises, but Roderick yanked free.

"*Don't* have my own butler cast me out!" he snarled. He whirled and stormed out the door, slamming it closed behind him.

Roderick fumed as he strode down the laneway. What was he going to do now? He had no money but the change in his pocket, no possessions but the clothes on his back. He wouldn't be able to replenish his funds, or reside on the estate, or enjoy the free benefits of a high renown. If he didn't find a source of income soon, he wouldn't be able to afford his apartment suite, let alone food. His life as it had been was at an end. But what stung more than being cut off from his family's resources was that his parents had been the ones to forsake him. He would've liked to think they'd be more supportive than that. Now that they'd gone through with it, though, there would be no convincing them to change their minds. He was on his own.

Then his thoughts went to Emmilene. How was he to marry her, when he could bring nothing to the table? He couldn't even buy her a proper wedding dress now!

Roderick returned to his apartment building, but was hardly surprised to find that he'd already been evicted, without even the chance to go up and gather any of his belongings, much less have any furniture relocated.

He slowly turned away and wandered through town.

He didn't even know how to go about getting a job. He tried stopping by the respectable establishments he used to frequent – the haberdashery, the bank, the law office – to see if they were hiring. But, of course, since he had no prior employment experience, none of them wanted him. Some recognized him as the recently disgraced libertine, and turned him down on that basis alone.

As the day grew late and he still had no luck, he realized he'd have to secure a place to stay before nightfall, or he'd be stuck on the streets. So he pawned his silver cufflinks, and used the money to pay half the first month's rent for a room at the cheapest apartment building he could find, which was all it would cover.

Roderick sat on the lumpy cot and looked around at the dingy room. He doubted he could even get to sleep in such a place. His spirit sank along with the deepening gloom.

Over the next few days, he went

hunting for jobs again, inquiring at progressively less dignified places of business until he'd exhausted all but his most desperate options. He returned to his apartment and sat in a rickety chair beside the desk, slumping in it glumly. How he wished he could afford a glass of gin right now.

Footsteps sounded in the hall outside the open door. Roderick lifted his head as Ishwar came by the doorway.

"Ah, how the wealthy have fallen," the lieutenant remarked grandly, striding ponderously into the room. "I thought it was about time your family knew the true nature of your character."

Roderick stared at him. *He* was the one who had done it? "Why?" he breathed. "Why are you doing this? I thought we were friends."

"We were. Until you dallied with my

sister."

Roderick's eyes widened slightly in dismay.

Ishwar cocked his head. "Did you think she wouldn't tell me?"

"Then why all this? Why not just force me to marry your sister?"

"Oh, I want better for Indira than a man like you. You'd just philander with other women behind her back. I needed to teach you a lesson." Slowly, he grew a smile that was almost fervid in its vindictive anticipation. "I'll make an honest man out of you yet."

Roderick was dazed. His life had been single-handedly ruined – by none other than his own lifelong friend, no less – but he'd brought it on himself. And all for what, a shameless dalliance he could just as well have avoided? He had no pride left. He had no money, no good name, no woman, and no prospect of getting any of it back.

Ishwar turned aside, flicking his leather gloves onto his palm. "So you're aware, Emmilene and I will be wed on the twenty-fifth of December." It was like the final blow to Roderick's heart. "However, there is one alternative – if, by that date, you can manage to earn two hundred pounds to buy the marriage license from me, and you bring that sum to the chapel by nine o'clock that morning, you can have Emmilene's hand in marriage." Then he went back out the door.

Roderick felt a ray of hope. There was a chance for him after all. If he had Emmilene, at least, maybe that would be enough to make his new circumstances bearable.

And then he had a realization. Marrying her would mean getting a dowry.

And it would be substantial compared to what he had now. The only way he could have a secure monetary future was if he married into a wealthy family – and that's what Emmilene's was. He'd considered them second-class before, but they were still considerably richer than he could ever hope to become by working a common job, even if he did it for the rest of his life. But first he had to earn enough for the license. Two hundred pounds – an amount he would've easily spent in a week in his old lifestyle. How hard could it be to make that much?

Roderick set out the next day, determined not to come back until he had acquired a job. He searched high and low for hours, until finally he found an opening at a place that would take him, at the sawpits in the southwest half of town, cutting boards for use in construction.

He started work there first thing the following morning, and was shown the ropes. Then he was assigned to the lower role down in the stone-walled pit, to cut long logs into planks with a two-man saw, while the more experienced top sawyer made sure to guide the blade straight. Even after the two of them finally established some semblance of coordination, it was still grueling work – messy too, with sawdust constantly sifting down around Roderick. It seemed to go on forever, with hardly a five-minute break every hour. Despite the October air, the sun beating down on him in the pit made him swelter just as much as the exertion.

When he came back to his apartment at the end of the day, he was covered in grime and smelled of sawdust. All his muscles ached; he'd never worked them so long or hard in his life. All he wanted to do was take a long hot bath – but even that was a luxury now, one that he couldn't afford more than once a week. He had to settle for a spongedown with a bucket of water heated in the fireplace.

Roderick was still sore the next morning, but he reported for duty again, and persevered for the rest of the week.

When he received his first salary, he was appalled at how meagre it was. All that work, and this is what he got for it? It was barely enough to buy a decent pair of boots! He used it to pay for his room and board, but there was hardly anything left after that. As the weeks went on, he calculated how much he'd earn over the next two months and how much of it he'd have to spend on essentials, and realized he wouldn't be able to save enough at this rate. He started cutting corners, no longer purchasing clothes to restock his wardrobe, and buying less food for himself – but that wasn't going to make enough of a difference, either. He'd never had to budget his expenditures this carefully before. He began working longer hours, even taking over shifts from the other workers.

Roderick was passing by his window one day when he glimpsed a familiar figure on the street below. A weight lifted from his chest. "Emmilene," he murmured. Cloaked in a satin hood, she darted across the road to his building and looked both ways down the sidewalk, then entered.

Roderick raced down several flights of stairs, and came to the dim foyer to find Emmilene pushing her hood back as she cast around. When their eyes met, glad yearning came over her face.

She hastened over to him and took his hands. "My family won't let me come and see you anymore, now that they know your reputation. I just barely managed to slip away."

Roderick was tired of playing by Ishwar's rules. His gaze became earnest. "Let's leave town together. Get married on our own terms."

Emmilene stared at him in wonder. Then her eyes saddened. "We can't run," she murmured. "You have no money. What will we live on?"

He lowered his eyes, dissatisfied, but resigned. "You're right. We have to do this the proper way." Then he met her gaze again with renewed determination, and held her face in his hands. "But I promise I'll get you back. I *will*." He looked into her eyes for another moment, then brought her over and kissed her. As always, once was never enough, and they soon became carried away. Roderick sank his fingers in her hair, and she looped her arms atop his shoulders, pressing herself against him. A familiar fire started up in him. He stroked a hand up the side of her slim waist, daringly close to her bosom.

Emmilene gave a faint moan, and set her hand on the side of his face, then pulled back from the kiss. "I can't stay long," she murmured with regret, eyes still closed. "They'll wonder where I am."

Pressing his lips together as he resisted the urge to kiss her again, Roderick leaned against her with his forehead, and drew her body snug to his with one hand. It would be so easy to take her up to his room so they could finish what they'd started... He wanted her so bad. "Just two more months," he reassured, and gave her one last ardent kiss.

Then Emmilene was turning away, and their hands stayed linked for another moment before she was out the door.

***

Emmilene stood gazing out the drawing room window, hugging her arms. It wasn't much of a view, from the upper floor at the back of her parents' townhouse. But her mind was elsewhere. She reminisced on her recent rendezvous with Roderick; how he'd smelled of sawdust, in a way that was still somehow enticingly masculine...how he'd felt even more muscular than before.

Boots clicked on the floorboards behind her as Ishwar came in. She turned to him, face troubled. "Why won't you call this off?" she pleaded. "I want to marry Roderick, and he wants to marry me."

The lieutenant's expression was sympathetic. "I know you didn't ask for this.

And I don't wish to cause you distress. But you must be patient. Either he'll get his act together in time, and you'll live blithely forever after – or he won't, and he never deserved to have you anyway. At least then, you'll still have a decent marriage to support you."

"But he *would* have married me, if he hadn't been stripped of his funds."

"That would've been too easy. He needed to be taken down a notch. 'In poverty and in wealth', after all. Even if he married you as easily as he's always gotten everything, there's no guarantee he'd stay faithful to you when times got tough. I'm merely grooming him to be a good husband to you." Ishwar showed a bit of a teasing smirk. "You'll thank me later." Then he turned and walked back out of the room.

Chapter 6

The partner Roderick was paired with at the sawpit was a lanky fellow with unkempt mousy hair and a wide mouth. Roderick didn't even catch his name the first few times, but he was quite the talkative one, often trying to engage Roderick in conversation or otherwise blithely chattering on for hours about everything under the sun, even over the sound of the rasping wood. Roderick for the most part tuned it out, rarely making – or needing to make – a response. He concentrated on thoughts of Emmilene, maintaining his determination to earn her back, just to get through the day's work.

But after a while, some of the details about the fellow's life began to sink in, and Roderick came to know him as Norrill Wexley. They began to share some dialogue, and gradually became friends. When he asked Roderick why he was so preoccupied, he told Wexley about Emmilene and how he'd have to earn enough to get her back. Wexley was enrapt and sympathetic, and wanted to do whatever he could to help, even recommending a part-time task that Roderick could do on the side for some extra money: unloading a cartful of barrels into a tavern every dawn and midnight. It didn't pay much, but neither did other odd jobs, and Roderick didn't have time for anything more than that. At least he got his wages on the spot, and he needed every bit he could get.

He kept it up through to the end of November, and his savings steadily grew, until he had over a hundred pounds.

The beginning of the month came around again, and so did his landlord, to collect his rent. Roderick pled with the man to grant him an extension, just until the end of December – since, if he paid it now, there was no way he'd have enough for the marriage license. After much reluctance, the landlord finally agreed, but only on the condition that Roderick would pay both months' rent first thing in the new year.

Then there was only a week left until the wedding, and Roderick feared he'd still be short by too much. Wexley offered him all twenty pounds of his own savings, meagre as they were. Roderick was astounded that a man with a wife and young children to provide for would give every spare penny he had to someone he'd only met a few months ago. It appeared some commoners were noble after all. Roderick assured him he'd pay it back as soon as he could; either the contribution would make his total amount to enough, and he'd marry Emmilene, whereupon her dowry would certainly cover the loan – or, if he still couldn't scrounge up the full two hundred pounds, he wouldn't be needing to use all of it anymore anyway.

Roderick started skipping meals, so as to spend that much less. Wexley was kind enough to share some of his work lunches with him, and even invited him to supper at his house, as often as Roderick could make it. The days almost blurred into each other; Roderick worked sixteen-hour double shifts, topped by his cask hauls, all the way up until the 24th.

It was late into the night when he finally got back to his apartments. He dropped his coin pouch onto the desk with a sigh. His last pay before the fateful day. It better be enough. He plunked himself down into the chair, and dumped out all his savings onto the table, to start slowly counting it up.

He'd hardly eaten – and slept even less – for days, and his mind was so drowsy and muddled it was hard to keep track of what he was doing, or if he was even doing it correctly, just from one moment to the next. Sometimes he stacked several banknotes without paying attention, and other times he was sure he'd assigned the wrong value to one of them, which made him backtrack to check, but that often confused matters further. He kept nodding off where he sat, only to jerk awake a second later, having forgotten what number he'd just gotten up to – so he had to start all over again. He never got very far. More than once, he did doze off entirely, often dreaming that he was still counting, so when he woke, he was certain he remembered the right amount – but that was impossible, since it was much too high; into the sixteen hundreds. He had no idea how long his naps lasted, but he went back to the task at hand with twice as much urgency to make up for it. Before he knew it, dawn was lightening the overcast sky out the window, and he still hadn't finished tallying it up. At least, he didn't think he had.

There was a brisk knocking on the

door, and then Wexley came right in without waiting for an answer. "It's quarter to nine!" he announced, then stopped short when he saw Roderick. "Why aren't you ready?"

"I'm counting," he mumbled without looking up. He paused. "Where was I?" His sluggish brain churned on that for a moment. "One hundred and ninety pounds and...eighteen pence?" Or was it eighty? No, it must have been eighteen. He went back to it, meticulously adding crowns together to make a pound, then shillings, then going penny by penny.

Wexley went to stand by the foot of the cot behind him and waited. Time dragged on.

"...thirty-eight, thirty-nine...forty." Roderick stared dully at the last penny. A hundred and ninety-nine pounds and forty pence. Could he really be short by only sixty pence? He groaned. If he had come that close, only to fail, he'd surely lose his sanity.

His soul was filled with anguished yearning. *Emmilene...!*

Arms sprawled over the tabletop, Roderick bowed his head and rested it on the wood. After a minute he muttered tonelessly to his friend, "Will you tell them that they've either broken my heart, or broken my mind?"

"Tell them yourself!" Wexley rallied, coming over to roust him out of the chair. "You've come too far to give up now. The wedding's in ten minutes! Just grab all you've got and let's hope it's enough!"

Roderick scooped all his hard-earned money into a sack, and then Wexley hustled him out the door. Roderick was still so tired, his friend had to guide him by the forearm to make sure he didn't stumble or bump into anything. They descended the staircases to the ground floor as swiftly as they could, and the rush of the moment made Roderick more alert. They hurried out onto the street to hail down a hansom cab; Wexley told the driver to make all due haste to the chapel, and they bucketed through town at a reckless gallop.

The cab pulled up in front of the flight of stone steps just as Emmilene and Ishwar were reaching the top, where the priest waited at his podium.

"Wait!" Roderick called, holding up the pouch as he ran up the stairs, trailed by Wexley. "Stay the ceremony!"

Emmilene turned, and her face bloomed into a smile of joyous relief to see that he had come. Ishwar wore a certain complacent look too.

Roderick arrived in front of the priest, panting, and offered the bag. "I've come to buy the marriage license from

Ishwar."

"Is this two hundred pounds?" the priest prompted as he took the pouch.

"I'm...not sure," Roderick admitted.

The priest poured the coins and banknotes out onto the podium before him, then started briskly adding it all up.

Roderick met Emmilene's eyes, which were as anxious and filled with yearning as his own must be. She looked so beautiful in her lacy wedding dress.

The priest began counting aloud as he neared the end. "One ninety-nine thirty..."

Roderick's heart pounded, and he hardly breathed as he anticipated the dreaded shortfall. How would he bear the expression on Emmilene's face when she realized he'd failed her...?

"...forty...fifty..."

Roderick looked at the priest in

surprise as he surpassed his own estimate. Then hope rose in his chest. Roderick himself must have miscounted. Maybe he really did have more than he thought!

"...ninety-eight...ninety-nine...two hundred pounds."

Triumph soared within Roderick. It was just enough!

The priest gathered all the money up into the bag again, then handed Roderick the marriage license. "It's yours to sign."

Roderick looked to Emmilene in wonder. Ishwar, smiling, graciously stepped aside to let Roderick come and stand by Emmilene instead.

She took Roderick's hand, gazing into his eyes. "Oh, Roderick," she breathed. "I knew you could do it."

He squeezed her hand – victorious, but still too exhausted to speak.

The priest opened the doors to lead the way into the dim chapel, and Roderick and Emmilene followed down the aisle together, with Ishwar bringing up the rear. The priest spread his hands as he passed between the guests seated on the pews. "There's been a slight change of plans," he declared. "The groom today will be Roderick Ruttledge."

There were several gasps and mutters, accompanied by creaking as people twisted around in their seats to look back at them.

The priest proceeded to the altar, and Roderick and Emmilene came to stand side-by-side facing him, while Ishwar took a seat on a front bench beside his parents.

The ceremony began with the usual speech, but Roderick barely heard. He was busy taking in the sight of Emmilene's face, imagining what it would be like once she was his wife. He didn't even care that he must look like a dishevelled beggar – and Emmilene didn't seem to mind either. He'd been waiting for this so long, he just wanted it to be official already.

Then it was time for the signing. The priest's assistant came over with a fountain pen and a small table that he set before them for Roderick to place the license on. As the priest spoke the words that they each replied to with "I do", Roderick signed on the lower left, then handed the pen to Emmilene, who wrote her name in an elegant script on the right. They turned to each other. Almost before the priest finished saying they were married, Roderick took Emmilene's face in his hands and kissed her, so passionately that there were some murmurs of surprised disapproval from the more decorous guests. So what if it wasn't part of the ceremony. She was his wife now. Several moments later, Roderick parted from a rather breathless Emmilene. She bit her lip, eyeing him with a coy smile. His gaze smouldered into hers. There was one thing he had been without for months, that he very much wanted to do with her, and only her.

The End

The Wizards'

Apprentess

Chapter 1

In the midst of a verdant forest, home to magic and enchantment, there ran a broad sparkling stream, over which gently arched a low, wide bridge of pale wooden planks. Crossing this bridge, as they often did on such pleasant midspring afternoons, were two wizards, wiry but spry for their apparent age, with long white hair and beards; Mezuthelion, in robes of green, and Zithemander, draped in blue. They had long been such good friends that they were akin to brothers, and now they worked together to train a new youth; their apprentess, Tayarene.

She wore a thick robe of deep plum purple, with sleeves as capacious as the others' - but somehow she still managed to make the garment look feminine and playful. For playful she was, more than any other apprentice they'd had, and though she was a bit of a handful, they fondly joined in her sport, as she was the light of their day. They bantered and chuckled and pranked and capered, as they headed home to their cottage in the eastern half of the woods.

But the second wizard, Mezuthelion, was lagging back, and now he cast an uneasy glance over his shoulder. He scanned the edge of the woods behind them, but still saw nothing.

Zithemander noticed him lingering on the bridge, and paused to call back lightly, "What delays you?" Their apprentess was already some distance ahead.

"Just keeping an eye out for the monster that's rumoured to be about," he responded absently.

The other wizard seemed to take it as a matter of course, turning back to accompany Tayarene, and assuming Mezuthelion would soon follow.

Eventually, Mezuthelion hesitantly trailed after them until he was off the bridge, but slowed once more to look back.

Then, from the shadows beneath the trees, it emerged: a large wolflike creature, but with fur of a dull purple upon its back, and a grey underbelly.

Mezuthelion saw it with some relief. "Finally," he muttered; he'd been worried it wouldn't arrive on time. Tayarene was almost out of sight around the bend. "This is the girl," Mezuthelion told the wolf, looking toward Tayarene.

The wolf turned his dark eyes onto her, where they fixed with intent interest.

"As I said before," the wizard added, "you mustn't let her know who you are." With that, he continued on to catch up to his companions.

The creature slunk across the bridge after them, and passed unseen back into the forest.

***

Tayarene skipped along, leading the way up the path to the cottage. It was a cosy one-storey home, just big enough for the three of them, with pale wooden walls and a hipped thatch roof sprouting a little chimney. She twirled, her thick braid of long brunette hair sweeping about, and waited for the wizards to catch up.

Mezuthelion was still trailing behind, so she called to Zithemander as he neared. "Is it time for potions practice yet?" she prompted eagerly.

Zithemander chuckled. "Dear girl, we've only just gotten back," he protested mildly.

"I know, but I've been waiting to start since before we left."

Mezuthelion came up and clapped a hand on Zithemander's back. "A restorative elixir and you'll be good as new." A lighthearted tease that Zithemander was the slightly older of the two.

"If only we weren't fresh out," Zithemander remarked.

"We might as well brew one up. Let's try it outdoors this time, shall we?" Mezuthelion suggested, and eyed Tayarene with a twinkle in his eye. "We don't want a repeat of what happened last week."

She put the back of a hand on her hip playfully. "You know very well I wouldn't have dropped that explosive mixture if that dusty spellbook of yours hadn't made me sneeze," she countered.

Smiling, the wizards started heading past her for the house, and she turned to accompany them.

"You should really make better use of that enchanted feather duster..."

The three of them went into the sunny little cottage and ferried all the supplies outside, starting with a long table on which they set an assortment of bottles. Then Zithemander instructed Tayarene on which ingredients to mix together in what order and quantity, and Mezuthelion monitored her closely as she obliged. Lastly, she poured the blue liquid of one rounded beaker into the other, sparking a delightful puff of purple smoke that wafted up.

"Splendid!" Zithemander exclaimed, then paused. "Now...who wants to test it?"

The two wizards eyed each other cautiously sidelong. There was no telling what an untested concoction might do.

"She made it for you, after all," Mezuthelion ventured.

"Oh, very well," Zithemander conceded. "But I'll conduct a scan first to check." He swept his hand over the opening of the bottle, but didn't seem to sense any toxicity. He took it up and downed it in a few gulps, and Tayarene watched with anticipation. He smacked his lips as he set it down. "Ah! Not bad! I can feel some of the vitality returning to me already." Tayarene relaxed with glad relief. "I believe it could use a touch more pepberry juice next time, though."

Tayarene thought she glimpsed a pair of dark eyes watching her from the forest edge, but when she looked, all she saw was a blackbird perched in a tree there, probably made curious by all the potions.

Once noon came, Tayarene went to a small nearby glade that was still draped in the shade of the forest. She sat crosslegged on the grass at the base of a tree, and snacked on her luncheon. Just as she was almost done, there was a faint rustle in the bushes ahead, and out hopped a little auburn squirrel. It cocked its dark eye at her, and she smiled at it warmly.

"Hey there, little guy," she greeted in a delighted murmur. It started hesitantly stepping its way closer in little fits and starts. "Looking for some treats?"

Tayarene prompted, and held out a nut of offering.

It made one more bound right to the brink of her folded shins, then straightened up and took the nut from her fingers with his little handlike forefeet. Then he crouched on his haunches there to nibble on the treat, just as if he wasn't in human company.

Tayarene was curious. Usually they leapt away a safe distance with their prize before starting in on eating it. "You're remarkably tame," she observed. She extended a gentle finger to stroke on its head; it stayed where it was and let her pet him.

It finished up the rest of the nut, then promptly climbed up onto her lap, but didn't seem to be looking for more food. Tayarene lightly ran her hand down the smooth fur of its arched back, a few times. She couldn't get over how friendly it was.

It scampered up her arm, then settled itself on her shoulder, its bushy tail - curled behind it - brushing the side of her neck. Tayarene watched it with a smile. She'd never been so close to a wild critter. She reached up and petted it some more, and it seemed content to stay there.

The enchanted whistle sounded from back at the cottage, announcing it was one o'clock.

Tayarene looked its way, then turned back to the squirrel. "Alright, I'm getting up now," she said to it. She slowly rose to her feet, and the squirrel braced itself with both forefeet on her shoulder. Then it jumped off to cling to the tree behind her, craning its neck to look around at her. She smiled back at it as she headed away. "See you around."

The next morning, Tayarene stood in the cottage with the wizards, concentrating her gaze on her open uplifted hand as she envisioned the wooden sphere in the other room and tried to conjure it. It was supposedly easier starting out over short distances. Finally, the sphere appeared in her palm, and she grinned.

"Well done!" Zithemander congratulated.

Tayarene noticed a green light out the west window, and turned her head to look. The orb on its post above the wooden message box - which was shaped like a little house - was slowly glowing on and off, to indicate someone in town had sent a note using the box's twin. "Oh, there's a message for you, Mezuthelion," she said.

"Ah. I'll get it right now, then."

He flourished his hand, and was suddenly holding the selfsame scroll, with a green string tied around it.

Tayarene looked on in amazement. "How'd you do that? You haven't even laid eyes on that scroll before!"

Mezuthelion smiled. "Yes, but I'm familiar with the location it was in. Once you become experienced enough in conjuring, it's just a matter of knowing where to summon from." He unfurled the scroll and read it. "It seems the cooper has misplaced one of his tools. It should be a simple matter to find it with a locating spell." Mezuthelion left the scroll on the table, then they headed out to town, even though they'd just been there the day before. Such was the nature of being the local wizards.

After a leisurely half-hour walk, they arrived at the quaint village, nestled in the woods, with its sturdy buildings topped by steep slate roofs.

They paused in the square, and Mezuthelion turned to Tayarene. "This should be a fairly routine task. You can sit this one out if you like."

"Why not let her come along?" Zithemander put in.

"She's seen us do the likes of it before. And there wouldn't be much for her to do, since we haven't started her on locating spells yet."

"I'll just pick up some things from the market while you're gone," Tayarene offered. "We used up all the clover yesterday anyway."

"As you wish," Zithemander acquiesced. "See if you can get some sparrow feathers too." He handed her a few coins. They parted ways, and Tayarene continued on to where several stalls lined the street outside the shops.

She drifted along until she came to a stand selling fresh goods. She looked over the display, then pointed out her selections to the vendor. "I'll have the clover, the garlic, and the...sparrow feathers."

"That would make for an unusual stew," someone remarked beside her.

Tayarene turned to find a lad a bit older than her standing there. He had raffish black hair and dark eyes, and was exceedingly handsome, in an appealingly boyish sort of way. His maroon tunic was cut in a crisp style, with a diagonal grey stripe from each shoulder meeting on the chest.

Tayarene smiled. "It's for a potion," she explained brightly. "I'm getting supplies for the wizards while they see to a client. I'm their apprentess."

"A wizard girl?" he repeated, a twinkle of genuine interest in his eye as he regarded her. "Very impressive. You don't see one of those every day." There was nothing mocking in his tone, only admiration.

"I know - witchcraft is the more popular choice, but wizardry doesn't take that much more skill." Tayarene accepted the burlap bag of produce from the merchant and paid him. She continued on past the lad, and he fell into step beside her as she browsed along the row of tables.

"You looking for anything else?" he prompted. "I know this market like the back of my hand. I do odd jobs for the merchants here. Just say Rizorian sent you, and they'll give you a discount."

"Actually, I *could* use some pixie powder," she admitted. "But I haven't been able to find any lately."

Rizorian squinted in thought. "Oh, yeah, I think I know someone who has some of that," he mused. "He mentioned he got a new batch of it just the other day."

They went to a shop past the stall at the very end, and Rizorian spoke with the merchant standing outside. As the man went in to get a sample, Rizorian looked at Tayarene. "Pixie powder, eh? That's used for love potions, isn't it?"

Tayarene chuckled, abashed. "It can also be made into a sleeping draught, of course, in the right combination."

When the merchant brought back a corked vial of sparkly dust, Tayarene thanked him heartily and gave him the necessary coins. Then she and Rizorian resumed walking.

Tayarene set the bottle in her bag,

and poked around in it to check if she had everything. "I...*guess* that's all I was going to get for now," she said, with a trace of regret.

They drifted to a stop, and Rizorian eyed her purchase bag. "You need to be getting back with those?"

"Neh, the wizards are using a locating spell to find someone's lost item. It could be a while."

Rizorian's eyes brightened a little.

"I should probably stay around here until they get back." She sat on the stone coping of a garden wall, the bag on her lap.

"I was thinking of staying around here too." He settled beside her.

Linking her hands around her knee, Tayarene leaned back and beamed up at the sky, where a hawk was gliding by high overhead. "The birds must have fun up there."

Rizorian looked over at her quizzically.

"Just imagine what it must be like, floating on currents of air. Levitation gives you some idea, but I'm not very good at it yet."

His eyebrows lifted. "Still, that's more than most people can do."

Tayarene chuckled. "True. It's not just birds that fascinate me, though. I admire animals of all kinds. They're so majestic and mysterious."

"Oh, absolutely," Rizorian agreed, turning toward her more. "Even though they can't speak, they still have emotions and personalities."

"Exactly! It would be unreasonable to think otherwise."

"And tame ones can be so affectionate. Sometimes I think they're more in touch with their true selves than people are."

She watched him avidly, nodding, enthralled that they had something so passionately in common.

"There's nothing quite like the freedom of running on four legs." Then Rizorian proffered a wry smile. "Or at least, so I imagine," he added.

"Tayarene!" Zithemander's voice called, and she looked over to see the two wizards coming up to them from a side alley. She was a little disappointed. She'd hoped it'd take them longer.

She looked back at Rizorian as she got up. "See you later."

He slowly bloomed into a hopeful grin. "Really?"

Tayarene paused in her steps to head away. "I mean, since you're often around in the market, and all," she explained haltingly.

His eyes still twinkled. "Right."

Chapter 2

Tayarene set out into the forest north of the cottage to look for plants with magical properties. She spotted a cluster of dandybloom, with their soft yellow flowerheads facing the sky. She went over and knelt by them to pick them one by one. Their five-inch stems were thick but hollow, and spongy enough to be easily plucked.

The underbrush nearby stirred, and out peeked a dark brown ferret. It regarded her, then came shuffling closer, to nose curiously at her handful of flowers.

"These?" she prompted. "They're

called dandybloom. I'm gathering them for a potion."

The ferret turned tail and scampered away. Tayarene watched it go. *Oh well.* Maybe it had been scared off by her voice.

She turned back to her foraging. But not a minute later, the ferret came lolloping back up to her, holding up a dandybloom in its mouth. Tayarene looked at it with amused surprise. It looked so cute, like a little animal suitor, with its little teeth just peeking out around the stalk.

"For me? Oh - why, thank you!" she remarked, accepting it to add to her collection. She stroked the ferret's head. "Aren't you a clever little creature." Its whiskers quivered in such a way that it looked rather pleased with itself.

Tayarene got to her feet to start looking for another patch, and the ferret went scouting around to bring back whatever dandyblooms it found. Someone must have trained it to retrieve things.

Whenever she was in the woods, she always met some little animal or other - an oriole, a rabbit, an auburn bobcat - who came up to her and kept her company like she was one of them. Tayarene reckoned she must just have an affinity for animals. That, or the ambient magic in the area had made all the wildlife more friendly.

One time, when she was practicing levitation by herself, a grey gull alighted in front of her and cocked its head. Tayarene thought it was an unusual animal to be found in a forest. But maybe it was a frequenter of the rivers and ponds in the area. With her hands held out slightly from her sides, palms facing down, Tayarene tried to will herself up, by generating a sensation of resistance in her core. As her feet lifted an inch off the ground, the bird spread its wings and flapped them once so it was briefly suspended in the air too. Tayarene chuckled. She couldn't maintain her hovering for long, but after she came down she tried again. The gull beat its wings a few times, staying aloft in place longer, and Tayarene decided to take it as encouragement, as if the bird was showing her how to do it. She managed to rise a full foot up, and stayed there for nearly half a minute - but then she had to lower herself again, because sustaining it felt like holding her breath. But she kept at it, and the gull continued motivating her, until she figured out how to actually move forward while she floated, whereupon the bird even took wing and flew around her, and Tayarene laughed with exhilaration.

The next time Tayarene was in town, she continued ahead to sell some extra dandybloom powder, while the wizards shopped elsewhere in the market. There she spotted Rizorian again, and he gave her a winsome grin as he came over.

"Did I catch you on your way out?"

Tayarene smiled. "I have one more stop I could make. At town hall, to hear what the latest news is." It was halfway across town; plenty of time for a nice stroll and a chat.

Rizorian fell into step beside her. "I'll walk you there, then." As they started heading along the street, he went on, "So, you live with the wizards? Do you have any relatives nearby?"

"My aunt identifies enchanted objects here in town. Magic runs in my family. She's the one that saw I had more potential in me than that, and encouraged me to achieve it by becoming an apprentess. So I had to relocate here, even though that means I'm far away from where my parents live. What about you?"

He shrugged. "I never knew my family. I guess you could say I'm an orphan."

Tayarene looked at him with concerned sympathy. "Oh. Sorry to hear that."

"It's not so bad. I was raised by a nice old craftsman, until he passed a year ago. Been on my own since then; moved here. I'm staying in a boardinghouse on the southwest side of town."

In a momentary lapse of discussion, they passed a boy gossiping to his friends. "I heard the monster will drag off anyone who enters the woods! And then he eats their souls!"

Tayarene turned away, shaking her

head.

Rizorian looked over at her. "Those rumours worry you?" he prompted.

"No, I just don't think the monster is as bad as all that."

He studied her consideringly.

They soon arrived at town hall: a square two-storey building made of grey stone bricks, with a flat roof. They joined a ring of townsfolk outside it and listened to the herald proclaim reports about local happenings, as well as notable tidings of neighbouring villages and lands. Tayarene and Rizorian, at the back of the gathering, muttered humorous comments to each other about each piece of news. After five minutes they turned to head back, since the herald would only repeat his accounts once every hour. On their way, they kept talking until the last moment, when

Tayarene could see the wizards in the market ahead; then she waved back to Rizorian as he stayed behind.

Every time she visited town, she met up with him again, and they often became immersed in riveting conversation about their shared enthusiasms. They talked about anything and everything; they laughed and shared updates about their days, and soon came to be close friends. They got along so well, and she really liked him.

One day, Tayarene was heading up the street, coming back from an errand the wizards sent her on to help with a client. She neared a circle of several youths her age, and overheard one of them saying, "You really think there's a monster, Suziri?"

Looking at them, Tayarene slowed to listen.

"Of course!" replied the blonde girl with her back to Tayarene. "There've been countless sightings of it. That monster has been terrorizing the town long enough. It's about time something was done about it."

Tayarene stepped in. "What makes you think it's a monster, and not just a regular animal?"

Suziri looked at her. "What else could it be, when it's a huge wolf with purple fur? It's undoubtedly vicious."

"When have you heard of it ever hurting anyone?" Tayarene countered.

"It matters not whether it's been seen attacking yet. It's an abomination. It needs to be eradicated."

Tayarene was taken aback by the extreme notion. "It's probably just some poor creature that's trying to mind its own business. You shouldn't judge it based solely on its unusual appearance."

Suziri sneered. "Taking the beast's side? You must be one of those sappy animal-lovers that wouldn't hurt a mouse even if it ate all the grain in your cellar."

Tayarene's mood darkened. "That's right, I wouldn't. There are humane ways to deal with inconvenient creatures. I'd cast a warding spell to keep it out of the cellar."

Suziri scoffed, turning back to the others. "Well, not all of us can just use magic to solve our problems. Sparing one mouse just leaves it free to raid someone else's cellar. *I* say, getting rid of that menace *before* it strikes would be doing everyone a favour." And she and her friends walked off before Tayarene could get a word in.

The apprentess balled her fists, stewing.

Chapter 3

Tayarene was passing by the message box the next day when she noticed its orb flashing red. *An emergency!* She rushed over to open the glass-paned door. Inside sat a small scroll tied with purple string, meaning it was addressed to her. She pulled the twine off and unrolled it.

Apprentess Tayarene,

Your aunt has become trapped in a magic sleeping mirror that can only be operated from the outside. No one else in town has the abilities to help.

Her stomach dropped. "Oh no,"

she breathed. The longer someone was in the mirror, the closer they would get to falling into an enchanted slumber. Tayarene looked around. Both of the wizards were gone foraging for herbs in the forest. It would take too long to go looking for them, or wait for them to get back. She set the scroll back in the message box and left its door open, so the wizards would notice it when they returned. She would have to go to town herself. But with the time it took to get there afoot, it might still be too late.

Just as she was wishing for a means of swift transport, a form stirred beneath the dappled shade of the trees, and out stepped a handsome stallion of a rich bay coat, watching her as it came to stand in the middle of the clearing. Tayarene stared at it for a moment, wondering what a wild horse could be doing out here in the woods - then she turned thoughtful. She carefully approached it, and stroked a gentle hand onto its velvety snout, which was received just as if it were a fully tame mount. She looked into one of those large, dark eyes. "Will you let me ride you?" Tayarene asked it in a whisper, and the stallion gave a decisive snort. Deciding to take her chances, she swung up onto its back, and nudged its side with her knee to set it charging onward to their destination.

Fifteen minutes later they galloped into town, and the horse clomped to a halt so she could dismount. Tayarene started striding purposefully in the direction of the boardinghouse, and the stallion trotted loyally after her. "Rizorian!" she called in desperation. She cast about for any sign of his face amidst those of the villagers, peering down alleyways as she went past. Without slowing, she even asked a passerby if they'd seen him around lately, but they hadn't. A blackbird flew overhead and disappeared behind the rooftops as she kept calling, "Rizorian!"

The lad himself suddenly emerged from a side street before her, looking surprised that she was calling him, but attentively concerned as to her urgent tone of voice. "What is it?" Oddly, he seemed somewhat out of breath.

Tayarene was so relieved to find him that she briefly set her hands on his chest as their meeting brought her to an abrupt stop. "It's my aunt! She's suffered a magical mishap! I need you to go get an anti-magic pendant from the market." Her aunt always wore one while inspecting unidentified artifacts to prevent these kind of incidents. But then that left the question, how had it happened?

"Of course," Rizorian agreed

earnestly.

Tayarene looked over her shoulder, but the bay stallion was no longer there. Frowning, she scanned around. "Where'd he go?" she wondered.

"Where'd who go?" Rizorian prompted.

"The horse that brought me here."

He paused for an uncertain moment. "Do you need a ride? I can get another mount for you -" he offered.

"No, never mind," she muttered. "I just thought he'd still be here when I need it."

Rizorian compressed his lips, with a very inscrutable expression of dissatisfied hesitation.

Tayarene looked at him again. "But go, hurry," she urged. "Meet me at my aunt's shop." She turned to hasten away, and Rizorian jogged off in the opposite direction.

She raced to her aunt's place and burst in the door. Inside the stand mirror ahead, her aunt looked up, then pressed her hands on the glass with an expression of desperate relief, and mouthed her name. Tayarene rushed up to her. "Aunt! Are you okay? How do I get you out?"

Her aunt frowned. Then her mouth moved, but no sound came through. Her aunt pointed to the frame, where there was a raised, carved disc. Then she made a turning motion with her hand. Tayarene tried to rotate the disc, but it wouldn't budge. Meeting her aunt's eyes, she shook her head and shrugged in a helpless gesture.

Her aunt pointed insistently to something behind Tayarene, then moved her hands like she was opening a book. Tayarene looked over her shoulder, and went to consult the volume laying open on the table there. It was a reference of antique magical objects, catalogued by her aunt, and it was open on the page about magic mirrors. Tayarene found the illustration of the particular kind her aunt was in, and read the notes on how to release a captive from it.

Rizorian came dashing in the open door, bringing the pendant to Tayarene. As she put it on, he caught his breath for a bit. He looked at her aunt in the mirror with concern, then turned to Tayarene. "Is there anything else I can do?"

"Looks like I'll need you to put this orb in that mirror frame at the exact same moment I turn the disc on the other side." She handed him the polished darkwood sphere she'd found on the tabletop.

She turned back to the mirror to see her aunt sitting sagged against the glass, blinking drowsily with her head nodding.

"No! Don't fall asleep!" Tayarene exclaimed. She wasted no time in starting the process. She rested one hand on the disc while she held the book in the other, and from it she read the incantation. "Segatsoh ruoy esaeler!" Just as she turned the disc to the right, Rizorian set the orb back in its socket. The glass became insubstantial, and her aunt slumped out. Rizorian darted to catch her under the shoulders before her head hit the floor.

Tayarene set the book down and knelt by her aunt, studying her face with worry, but her aunt's eyes remained closed. "Come on, Aunt, wake up," she pleaded, lifting her aunt's hand in hers and patting the back of it. But she didn't stir.

Rizorian looked up at Tayarene for instructions.

She ran a hand back over her own hair, staring at her aunt. "I'll have to make an antidote potion," she muttered. *Even though they don't always work.* "Let's get her on the bed."

Tayarene took her aunt's ankles while Rizorian hefted her up under her back, and together they shuffled her over to the cot by the side wall. They made sure she was laid out comfortably - then Tayarene went bustling about gathering supplies, bringing them back to the table to start mixing them together in a very precise sequence and measure. She had Rizorian help out when he could, fetching bottles from the shelves or holding things when she needed more than two hands. He obliged silently so as not to break her concentration, and mostly watched her work, solemn yet fascinated; but once she caught him looking at her with deep admiration.

When she was finally done, she took the blue potion over and held it near her aunt's nose so she would breathe in the billowing vapour. After a full minute, Tayarene withdrew the bottle and waited with bated breath. But even after several minutes, there was no change. “It's not working,” she whispered. She got a sinking feeling. What if she hadn't done the potion right? She'd never had to make one for something this important before.

“Maybe it just needs more time to set in,” Rizorian suggested.

Tayarene nodded, setting the bottle on the bedside table. “You're right. Some enchanted sleeps take longer to wake from than others.” She tried to calm her nerves by reminding herself of that.

She leaned back on a low bureau with her hands on the edge, watching her aunt. Rizorian came over to settle likewise beside her. After a while, he set his hand on top of hers. A poignant tenderness rose in her. Tayarene interlaced her fingers with his. She was very grateful that he was staying with her in her time of crisis, just to be there for her. He was a true friend.

The better part of an hour passed, but still her aunt showed no signs of coming to. Then the grand clock behind them chimed noon, and Tayarene looked over her shoulder. She turned to Rizorian. "Do you need to have luncheon?" she prompted.

He met her eyes. "I'd rather stay."

She smiled. "If nothing's happened in an hour, it's not likely to anytime soon. I'd feel better if I knew you'd eaten."

Rizorian hesitated for another moment. "All right. But I'll bring you back something." He rose and went out the back.

A few minutes later, the sound of Mezuthelion calling her name carried through the open front door. Tayarene leapt to her feet and ran outside.

The two wizards came hustling up the street. "We came as soon as we found the message," Zithemander said, taking her hands.

"I didn't get her out soon enough," Tayarene lamented as they went inside. "I gave her an antidote, but she still hasn't woken."

The wizards crossed to her aunt's bedside, and Zithemander hovered his hand over her forehead to perform a magical assessment, while Mezuthelion double-checked with Tayarene that she'd made the potion with all the right ingredients.

"You did well," Zithemander told her. "There's nothing more to be done now, but wait for the potion to take effect."

Tayarene wrung her hands, monitoring her aunt. "I should stay here with her, until I know she's alright." If she didn't wake, it would mean Tayarene's potion hadn't been effective after all, and the wizards would have to administer another one - but by then, more time would have passed, and it would be all the harder to revive her at all.

"Shall we remain with you?" Zithemander offered.

She paused. "No, you don't have to. I'll be alright."

Mezuthelion set a hand on her back. "You're sure?"

Tayarene nodded. "I'll send you a message if I need anything."

Zithemander patted her shoulder as they headed past her for the door. "Take heart, dear girl. All will be well."

Once they'd left, Tayarene sighed and pulled up a chair beside her aunt's bed. Leaning on her knees, she clasped her hands and set her chin down on her fingers, eyes steady on her aunt. She was going to stay here overnight if she had to.

Chapter 4

The band of black-clad youths chased the monster through the dark forest, only catching fleeting glimpses of it between the trees; a flash of purplish fur here, a swish of tail there. They fired arrows at it whenever they got a chance, but aiming at a barely-seen moving target at night, while running, rarely yielded more than a hit trunk or pierced ground. One time, however, after a shot flew out of sight, a yip of pain sounded from the blackness ahead.

"I think I nicked it!" the lad responsible yelled triumphantly.

The rest of them kept charging forward in anticipation, and broke out into a moonlit clearing - but there was no sign of the monster. They straggled to a halt in the middle of the open space, casting about everywhere, and several of them fanned out to search the treeline. In the ensuing silence, Suziri listened hard for any hint of its presence, and heard a faint swishing within a pond on the right.

"What was that?" she demanded, pointing imperiously.

One of her boys knelt down by the pool's edge, and leaned forward on his hands to peer into the water. "It's just a fish," he reported dismissively.

"It might have seen the monster go by," Suziri reckoned. "Let's take it to the town witch and have her scan its memory." It was a long shot, but she would take any lead she could get. Their hunt was at an end anyway; there would be no finding the monster again tonight.

***

Tayarene was strolling down the main street of town, hands in the capacious pockets of her robe. Waiting for her aunt's situation to improve kept her anxious, and she hadn't been able to sleep. She glimpsed a motion ahead, and glanced up in time to see a stream of dark-clothed figures dash across the street. She frowned, and hurried after them to see what was going on. She rounded the corner into a narrow side alley, and as she got closer to them, she recognized the blonde girl bringing up the rear.

"Suziri!" the apprentess barked, and the girl glanced sharply over her shoulder. She held a clear glass canteen of water with a small orange fish swimming in it, and several of her young cohorts had ebony bows slung across their backs. Tayarene didn't know what they were up to, but by the looks of it, it couldn't be anything good.

"Stay back, animal lover!" Suziri disparaged scathingly. Her team of about twelve had paused by the roofed back porch of a bungalow, and now she followed them in scaling up the porch's fence-pillar, onto the roof tiles of the house.

The apprentess caught up to where they had been, and unthinkingly scrambled up after them. She started chasing the gang across the low slope of the slate tiles, but by that time they were already halfway across.

They ran up a plank that led to the flat rooftop of a two-storey shop, which stood several yards away from the building they were on. When the last one had crossed, he kicked the board off so it fell to the cobblestones below with a clatter that jarred the complacent stillness of the night.

Tayarene lifted her arms from her sides and rose into the air, levitating herself across the gap to land on the rooftop. She pursued them across it, but Suziri turned back to face her just short of the edge, and Tayarene paused too, still in a ready stance.

"That monster deserves to be put down," the girl called heatedly. "You won't stop us!" She cast the jugful of water, fish and all, into the square planter in the corner. Then she whirled after her posse and leapt off the building, dropping from sight.

The apprentess rushed after her,

and stopped at the ledge to peer over it, down at the dark street below - but the lot of them were nowhere to be seen. Then Tayarene hastened to check on the fish, which was still moving, in a small puddle that had accumulated in the corner of sunken dirt. With a wave of her hand she conjured a jar out of thin air, and carefully scooped the fish up into it. She was skilled enough by now that she could summon it all the way from her aunt's house. “Don't worry,” she murmured to the fish. “I'll get you back home.”

Tayarene went to the north side of the roof and stepped off the edge, holding one hand out to float down until her feet touched the ground. Then she headed east out of town, and held up a glow-orb to light the way on her fifteen-minute walk to the stream. There she knelt and poured the fish into the dark waters.

~~~

Tayarene straightened in her chair and rubbed her eyes. Morning sunlight streamed into her aunt's shop, but her aunt still lay there on the cot. Tayarene was about to look away when she thought she saw her aunt stir. Then her aunt inhaled and opened her eyes. Tayarene's heart leapt.

"Aunt!" Tayarene cried, springing up to sit on the bed by her aunt's side as she levered herself up. "I was afraid my antidote hadn't worked!"

Her aunt wrapped Tayarene in an embrace. "Oh, I had no doubt you could do it."

Tayarene backed up to look at her. "How did it happen? You're always so careful. Why weren't you wearing your
~~~

anti-magic pendant?"

"It's the strangest thing," she mused. "I haven't been able to find it lately. I found my window open one day, when I hadn't left it that way. I think some hooligans broke in and stole it. But what they'd want it for, I don't know."

The first thing that came to Tayarene's mind was Suziri and her gang. Could they have taken it to use as a precaution against the monster, even though there was no reason to believe it could use magic on anyone? She felt a flare of indignation. She wouldn't put it past them, what with them sneaking around at night in their dark garb. She just couldn't recall if she'd seen Suziri wearing one. But if they'd put her aunt through all that peril just for their baseless vendetta... Tayarene had to tell the wizards about them. Someone had to make sure they didn't continue their mischief, especially if they were going to be terrorizing innocent animals like that fish in the process, for whatever purpose.

Tayarene met her aunt's eyes again. "Couldn't you have gotten another pendant at the market?"

"They didn't have any the last time I checked. And that mirror's been on a rush order for days, as requested by its owner. Besides, we used to identify without them, back in the old days before anti-magic pendants were made. It's always been a risky business."

"Well, here, have this one," Tayarene offered, lifting her own pendant off and settling it over her aunt's head instead. "I'll see if I can find out what happened to yours."

Tayarene checked to make sure her aunt was all back to normal now, with no narcoleptic side effects from the enchanted sleep. After she helped her aunt get settled and saw if she needed anything, her aunt told her she'd be fine.

Tayarene went to the message box at the east end of town and wrote a quick note to the wizards.

My aunt's awake, and doing well! I'll be heading back soon. Tell you more when I get there.

Tayarene

After she sent it, she started off toward the market to look for Rizorian. She spotted him in the midmorning crowd with his back mostly to her, and headed for him.

He turned his head her way, and she was alarmed to see a thin cut running across his right cheek. "Rizorian!" she breathed, hurrying over to him. She lifted a hand to hover near it, but he winced and averted his face as if belatedly trying to hide it from her. "What happened?"

"It's just a scratch," he explained lightly, with a bit of a grimacing smile. "Hunting accident."

She met his eyes curiously. "I didn't know you hunt."

"I don't," he admitted, but she was too preoccupied with her concern for him to bother with puzzling out what that meant.

"Here, let me mend it for you," Tayarene murmured. She took a small orb of smooth aquamarine out of her robe, and rolled it between her cupped palms until it glowed with healing power. Then she raised one hand and lightly touched her fingertips to just below the wound, conveying the magic to it. It closed up in a matter of seconds, leaving only smooth skin in its place, and she lowered her hand in relief.

Rizorian's mouth promptly spread into a more customary insouciant beam. "Thanks!" he remarked brightly. "I knew you wouldn't let anything happen to such a pretty face."

Tayarene smiled easily too, and tucked the sphere away again. "Anyway, I should be getting home now, but I just came to say my aunt is fully recovered."

"Oh! Great! See, I told you there was nothing wrong with your potion." The day before, Rizorian had come back after lunch and kept her company for a few more hours, but then Tayarene had reassured him that he didn't have to spend the whole day there. He must've gotten the scratch sometime between then and now.

"Oh, and I forgot to reimburse you for the pendant you got for me," she added, starting to dig out a coin from her pouch.

But Rizorian waved the thought away. "Nah, don't mention it! It was the least I could do."

Tayarene paused, then smiled again. "Well, thanks so much for all your help," she finished warmly. "It means a lot." Rizorian just kept looking at her gently with a faint smile, and she wondered if he was thinking about how they'd held hands, and what that meant to her. She turned to go before she could become bashful. "See you."

Once she was on the eastward path into the woods, she kept it in mind to tell the wizards about Suziri. When she neared the cottage, they came outside to meet her.

"There's a gang of young hunters in town," Tayarene told them urgently as she ran up. "They're going after the creature they call the monster." They both looked concerned - but it might have been more for the youngsters doing the hunting than for the monster. "We have to do something to get them to stop."

The two exchanged a deliberative glance. "Our assistance hasn't been requested in this matter," Zithemander replied regretfully. "It is not our place to interfere."

As he turned and left the conversation, Tayarene appealed to the other one. "Mezuthelion," she pleaded.

He started heading past her too, but in the direction of town. "Worry not, child," he murmured with an absent pat on her arm. "I will see to it that no harm comes of this."

Her face warmed into a smile of grateful relief. Then she followed

Zithemander inside to fill him in on the details of her aunt's recovery.

Mezuthelion was gone for several hours, but as the afternoon became late, Tayarene went out and sat on a stump to watch for him, too expectant to do anything else.

When she finally saw Mezuthelion returning, she got to her feet and hastened to meet him. “How'd it go?”

“Suffice it to say, I led them to believe that the monster had moved on to another town. They were so zealous in their goal that they relocated themselves there. I doubt we'll be hearing from them again.”

Tayarene broke into a grin, and hugged the wizard sidelong.

Chapter 5

As Tayarene stepped out of the cottage, the message box orb glowed purple. *For me?* Tayarene hurried over to check it. She undid the purple twine and unfurled the scroll, to see it was from Rizorian. Her heart warmed at the thought of him.

Been a few days since I saw you. Just felt like chatting. Figured, why wait, when I could send a message? I was just wondering, what do you think would happen if you took a sleeping potion right after a levitating potion? Would you end up sleepfloating?

Tayarene grinned. Then, feeling playful, she took a slip of parchment from the enclosed compartment beside the box and wrote a reply of her own with a peacock-feather quill, which was enchanted so it never ran out of ink.

Actually, it might give you dreams of being suspended on clouds.

She closed the door to send it through, and it disappeared in a flash of light. She waited around for a few minutes, bobbing on her toes, hoping Rizorian was still there at the town message box to see it. Sure enough, a second scroll soon showed up.

What, you mean mixing potions can give you sweet dreams on demand? Then give me a youth potion and I'll sleep like a baby!

Tayarene giggled, then composed another response.

***

The two wizards stood some distance behind, watching their apprentess.

"She's been messaging for over an hour," Zithemander muttered. But there wasn't much emphasis in it.

Mezuthelion was smiling fondly. "Ah, let her enjoy it," he murmured.

***

Tayarene sat at the base of a tree after luncheon, in the same clearing she often frequented.

An auburn fox trotted out into the open. Its paws were black, as were its ears and the tip of its bushy tail. It idly nosed at the ground a bit, then came padding over to her, and settled itself onto its haunches in front of her.

The apprentess smiled. "You're quite well-mannered." She stroked her hands over the fluffy fur on either side of its face, studying it thoughtfully. "You remind me so much of another creature," she murmured.

It gazed at her for a moment with those dark eyes, eyes that she was sure she had seen on every other animal she'd met with lately... Then she watched as the fox morphed before her eyes, into that very same auburn squirrel she had just been thinking of. Tayarene drew in a soft gasp. They weren't just wildlife, none of them; it was a single creature, that could change its form at will, into anything that was part of the animal kingdom. But what kind of creature could do that?

"What *are* you?" she whispered.

The squirrel's tail twitched. It turned and scurried a few feet away before facing back to her. Then its form changed and grew, until there stood before her a wolflike creature the size of a bear, with purple and grey fur. Tayarene's mouth slowly dropped open. The creature everyone called the 'monster'.

But wait...that meant her animal friend and the monster were one and the same. Yet, in all its forms, it had been so playful and friendly and harmless, even helpful. He could've changed into the monster at any time and attacked her when she was vulnerable, but he never had.

Then Tayarene's face bloomed into a grin. "I knew you weren't a monster!" she cooed. "You're just a shapeshifter!" Encouraged by her response, he came back over, and laid himself out before her. "For all we know, you could have the spirit of a mouse!" He set his muzzle down on her knee, looking up at her with endearing eyes. She stroked his head between the lowered ears. "You wouldn't hurt anyone, now would you?"

He nuzzled against her midriff, and Tayarene wrapped her arms around his shaggy neck, hugging him close and snuggling her face into his warm thick fur.

No wonder those animals had all been so familiar with her. They'd already known her from before! This meant every moment she'd spent with them, all the fondness of each interaction, she could now attribute to one individual!

From then on, since she knew what the creature could do, he often changed into different forms on the spot, and Tayarene had even more fun with that.

On one occasion, she ran around with him trotting as a fox by her side. When she tossed a kerchief into the air, he turned into an owl in mid-stride and flew ahead to catch the cloth in his talons, then banked and came gliding back to her. As she took the kerchief, he alighted on her arm, then morphed into that same dark-brown ferret. Smiling, Tayarene held him close and nestled her cheek against his furry little face. He was an animal companion like she'd always wanted - but even better than just a pet, because he could shapeshift into all kinds of creatures. And because he was her friend.

One afternoon, Tayarene went down to the stream wearing only a linen top and shorts, so she wouldn't get her robes wet. She waded calf-deep into the cool current and bent over, reaching a hand in to look for fish scales amidst the smooth pebbles of the riverbed.

On the opposite bank, a dark brown otter bounded over, and rose up on its hind legs with its forefeet tucked on its chest.

Tayarene met its merry dark eyes, and smiled. "Hey there, you," she greeted. It seemed that no matter where she went, she'd never be without company.

The otter promptly dove into the water, did a few fluid twirls, then bobbed back up, looking at her expectantly.

"I can't play right now, I have collecting to do," she protested lightly.

The otter floated around on its back, chittering playfully.

Tayarene chuckled. "Oh, all right, just for a little bit!" she conceded, and went splashing after the otter. They chased each other around, sometimes with Tayarene swimming too. Or she floated on her back and the otter made a swimming jump right over her middle. He even climbed up on her, and she stroked his wet fur, then hugged him.

But, much as she enjoyed their romps, eventually she had to get back to the task at hand. So as to spend that much more time with her, the otter helped her gather what she was looking for, as it had before, since it was clearly even more intelligent than a regular animal. She welcomed his companionship, and wished it could be for the whole day. His assistance must mean he cared about her.

Every time Tayarene headed to town with the wizards, she looked forward to meeting with Rizorian. She was always glad to see him, with his handsome face and cheery expression. They were even closer now after the episode with her aunt. They also started going to events like craft festivals and potion contests, in which case Tayarene stayed longer while the wizards continued home. By the time she'd known Rizorian for three weeks, it was like they'd been best friends for years.

Upon parting with him one time, Tayarene turned and started away, harbouring an ebullient smile. A warm glow of affection still filled her heart. Could it mean...she was in love with him? She was in reverent awe of the possibility. This was the first time she'd ever felt like this about someone!

One hot summer day, Tayarene went to her favourite skinnydipping pond in the forest. She stopped by the edge and peeled her robes off over her head, letting them drop in a crumple to the ground beside her. Then she slowly lowered herself into the lukewarm water, which was cooler than the air by just enough to be refreshing. She continued in until her whole bare body was submerged, with just her head above, as she lazily stirred her arms. It sure beat all the work of drawing a bath.

The surface rippled nearby, and a little orange fish poked its head up. Tayarene was delighted to see it. It was the same fish she had rescued from Suziri. And now she recognized its twinkling dark eyes. "That was you, too?" It was a good thing Tayarene had helped it. He probably hadn't wanted to morph into a different animal in front of the hunters, lest he reveal his identity. Suziri must not have known she'd had the very 'monster' she was seeking, right in her grasp!

The fish ducked under again, and soon Tayarene thought she could sense the slight swishing of its passage through the pool around her.

She felt something small and warm and smooth brush very lightly across the sole of her foot, then her right thigh...then her waist...and arm, and hand, exploring her naked body little by little. It felt very sensual, and somehow she got the feeling that the fish intended it that way, and was enjoying her sultrily too.

Tender feelings stirred within Tayarene, and she wondered; how could she be in love with an animal? But she felt a deeper connection with it, as if its soul was more than just that of a creature.

The fish resurfaced in front of her, eyeing her softly as it slowly drifted around her. Then it morphed into a sea lion, and Tayarene stroked a hand over its sleek back as it glided past.

She remembered Rizorian, and felt a bit of a guilty twinge. How could she feel as much for the creature as for him? It wasn't fair to either of them. Neither knew she was always meeting with one behind the other's back; each probably thought they were her only special friend. They'd never been in the same place at the same time before. Maybe she should tell them. But what would Rizorian think, if she said she had feelings for an animal? It wasn't like she could choose the creature instead of a human. And would the shapeshifter be hurt, if it thought she was favouring a person over it? She didn't know what to do. But she couldn't stop seeing either of them without explanation, not until she decided.

Chapter 6

As the summer went on, Tayarene continued to visit the forest's many waterways in her swim clothes, just for fun and cooling off. She was invariably joined by her animal friend, who often changed into a dolphin, as it seemed that was one of his favourite forms. It was one of her favourites, too. They swam together in the streams, which were just deep and wide enough for him to be afloat in. Tayarene sidestroked alongside him, or behind his fluke, or sometimes held onto his dorsal fin so she could drift along with him as he glided through the water. When they reached larger ponds, they played around more rambunctiously, splashing each other and doing tricks and even maneuvering underwater. They were like two dolphins in a pod.

Late one afternoon, after spending hours with him, Tayarene idled near him in a secluded pond. The air, thick with pleasant heat, was gradually cooling, the sun just beginning to turn ruddy as it reflected off the calm rippling surface.

The dolphin gradually drifted over to her, sidling his rounded beak in over her shoulder, and Tayarene tenderly wrapped her arms around his barrel, just above the flippers, as if they were sharing a real hug. He slowly stirred his fluke, tail curved so they started rotating in place, floating together in the warm water. Gently Tayarene closed her eyes, resting her head on the side of his, letting herself be carried in the tranquil moment.

Then, she heard a very quiet sound; that of a soft, young male voice, as if it was whispering by her ear - or in her mind.

If only I was in my human form, and able to speak... it mused absently to itself, wistful. *Then I could tell her how much I love her... If only she could hear me...*

Tayarene was filled with excitement as she realized she must be tuning into his thoughts. "But I *can* hear you!" she told him in hasty reassurance, and the dolphin backed up to look at her in wonder.

You can? There was a sparkle of hope in that dark eye. But then its expression turned solemn. *Then...there is something else I must tell you.* His mental tone was heavy with regret. *I only have a few hours left to live.*

Tayarene stared at him, feeling her stomach drop with dreadful shock. "What?" she breathed.

He lowered his eyes. *I will soon perish unless I find the kiss of true love; I only had till I turned eighteen. That time will be upon me any hour now.*

Her eyes began to mist with tears. "Oh, my dear friend!" she whispered. Would that she or the wizards could lift his spell, but she knew that whatever required true love's kiss had no such loopholes. Then she had a thought. "Wait - let me do it! You can turn into your human form, right?"

I already begin to weaken. He was looking increasingly weary, his head low in the water, his eyelids half-closed. *I'm unable to transform now, unless I come to be on dry land.*

"Then here, let me help you ashore!" she offered with alacrity, hastening back until her feet had a purchase on the soft floor of the pond, while using her hands, still on his flippers, to tow him afloat through the water. She assisted in pulling him up onto solid ground, until he was beached fully out of the shallows. He lay there inertly, and Tayarene knelt by his side to watch and wait with worry, while her wet clothes and braid dripped onto the sand.

As the sun dried his skin, his form began to shift and change - until there lay on his back a clad human lad whom she instantly recognized.

What delight, what relief, to see that he was none other than Rizorian! All her guilt was banished, for her two loves were one!

He smiled faintly at her expression.

"Surprise," he murmured.

Of course; the voice of his thoughts had sounded familiar, but she had just been too caught up in the urgency of the moment to make the connection. And those dark eyes were the same, with their dear sweetness, with their knowing twinkle. She was sure now that she would make a viable candidate for the task, for it was clear that not half, but all of her heart belonged to him.

Tayarene set her hands on the sand before her knees, regarding his recumbent form. "Here goes," she murmured.

Then she slowly leaned down, hovering over his face, and sidled her mouth up to his to give him a very tentative, inexperienced kiss. His lips were a bit cold, and still wet from the water, but her heart sang to be so close to him, to be connected with him that way - and though he was still too weak to move much, she could tell he felt the same avidity to stay united with her.

When she backed away, she studied him anxiously. “Did it work?” she whispered.

“No it didn't,” he murmured, resigned.

“Of course it did!” she insisted with bolstering conviction. “It must have!” She paused, then repeated more tenuously, “Right?” At least, she really hoped so. She felt a trace of uneasy doubt now. If it hadn't, that meant that they weren't really meant for each other...and that would be beyond devastating. Even worse, it would mean he had no one near that could save his life on time - and then he would be gone, and...her love for him couldn't stand that painful thought.

"Maybe we should...try it again," Rizorian muttered, voice still faint. "...just to make sure."

She was all too keen to oblige, if it would increase the chance of success. So she bent down with her forearms laid against his chest, and kissed him again, with all the concerned affection she felt inside - but from there, it turned into a lengthier thing.

Rizorian absently wrapped his arm around the back of her shoulders, tilting with her slightly to one side. Held close atop him, Tayarene could feel all the adolescent muscles of his chest and torso and arms, surrounded by his warm body. He now participated actively in the leisured kissing, as reluctant to leave off her lips as he was eager to hold onto them again. He certainly seemed to have his vitality back now.

When finally they parted again, he was looking at her with eyes as full of life and spirit as ever.

"Are you restored?" Tayarene hoped softly.

There was a twinkle again in his dark eye. "Most entirely," he asserted with quiet complacence.

She was filled with glad relief. "So it wasn't ineffective after all," she remarked, then eyed him sagaciously. "Did you just say that to get me to kiss you again?"

He grew a slight smile. "Maybe."

She scoffed incredulously, lightly flapping the back of a hand on his chest. "Don't scare me like that," she protested in a murmur. But she was smiling too, and their eyes still met tenderly, with their faces so near.

"I just needed an extra dose of

you," he confessed softly.

Her heart glowed with warmth, and she nestled her head contentedly on his shoulder. It was a great comfort to know, with the utmost certainty, that theirs was a match of true love. Their success in averting the spell served as irrefutable proof.

Then she turned thoughtful. "But, if it was you all along...how did you find me?"

Rizorian paused with a wry quirk to his mouth. "Mezuthelion pointed you out to me."

Tayarene glanced at him in surprise. Mezuthelion had been in on it?

"He and I have known each other for years. I told him about my curse, and he set to work trying to discover the one who could break it. Turns out, it was you. I couldn't tell you, or it might have changed whether you developed any feelings for me naturally."

"Why did you come to me in your animal forms first?"

"You needed to know every side of me," he explained. "To love me for all that I truly was. Otherwise, the kiss might not have worked."

"Then how come you never changed into an animal before me?"

Rizorian was sober. "It was all those rumours of the monster. A person shapeshifting into a creature might've seemed all too alarming. I didn't want to scare you off."

Tayarene smiled teasingly. "I don't scare easy."

Rizorian smiled, too. "I know that, now." He stroked the back of a finger up and down her bare shoulder. "I might've guessed, what with you chasing after hooligans and such."

Little had she suspected that the fish she'd saved had actually been Rizorian! Now that she thought about it, if she hadn't pursued Suziri, she might not have dumped the fish as a distraction. "I'm so glad those hunters didn't get to you," she murmured. She wouldn't only have lost her animal companion, but the human love of her life.

Rizorian drew her a little closer. "I have you to thank for that," he said softly. "And so much more."

Now that the sun had dried their clothes and warmed them, they sat up and rose to their feet. They started strolling homeward, and Rizorian sidled his hand over to hold hers. Tayarene linked her fingers with his.

"Thanks for helping me figure out levitating, by the way. It really came in handy."

"Well, if you ever need a wizard's familiar," he began playfully, "you know where to find me."

Untouched

Chapter 1

Cerieda was a beautiful princess. Though she was only a child, she was already among the fairest in the kingdom, with her silky golden tresses and gentle green eyes. She was kind and sweet, with grace of character and an innocent nature for which she was beloved by all. As she turned thirteen and began to blossom into womanhood, it became clear that she would only become more lovely with time. Because of this, her father worried for her safety, knowing well the selfish hearts of men. Thence he commissioned her grandfather, a great shaman, to cast a spell of protection over her; this he did while waving a ceremonial staff over her head.

Quoth he,

" 'She shall not be disrobed against her will,

By any man who wish her ill;

Only he with purest heart and intent,

Truest love or heavensent,

May touch her so if she concurs,

That man whose love will be hers.' "

Cerieda felt a cool prickling settle around her like a second skin. In a trice it was gone. Other than that, she didn't feel any different. She went over the words again in her mind, trying to work out what exactly they entailed. Did that mean the spell would physically repel the touch of everyone but her true love? Or only those who had the wrong intentions?

A few weeks later, a debutante ball was held in the palace to celebrate her coming of age. Young princes and princesses from all across the land were invited.

Cerieda stood in front of the full-length mirror in her dressing room, tying her sash. There was a knock on the door.

"Are you ready, Cerieda?" her father called through the wood.

"Just about," she replied, and set her diamond-studded tiara on her head.

She went to open the door, and joined the king in the hall. Even on formal occasions he didn't wear regal robes, simply his usual long coat of embroidered maroon velvet. His crown was a modest band of gold inlaid with a few rubies.

As they turned and headed down the corridor, Cerieda wondered, "If you don't want boys to meet me, why make my appearance at a dance at all?"

"It's not that I don't want them to get to know you," her father said. "I just don't want them trying anything they shouldn't." He gave her a smile behind his short brown beard. "Besides, I do want you to have a good time. You still can, without there being any touching."

The king entered the grand hall first while Cerieda waited outside. Then, a few moments later, she made her entrance into the spacious room, where dozens of brightly-dressed youths were gathered. She was announced by a herald, and the guests greeted her by bowing. Once she'd joined the crowd, the band began playing courtly music.

A slim, sandy-haired prince came up to her and bent at the waist. "Care to dance?" Though his words were polite, his face was set.

She smiled at being asked. "Certainly." They went to the middle of the ballroom floor and faced each other.

He set a hand on her waist, but jerked it back immediately, flapping it in pain. "Ow! I sprained my wrist!" Grimacing, he rubbed it with his other hand.

Cerieda withdrew her hands together in front of her bodice, concerned. "Sorry," she murmured. "It must be the spell Grandfather put on me." Even though the prince had only been assuming the dance form, and it hadn't been without her consent.

The boy looked up at her with a frown. "The what?"

She lowered her eyes, soberly smoothing her skirts. "We can only dance together if we don't touch," she said in an even smaller voice.

He eyed her very oddly sidelong and drifted off – probably to find a less weird partner, or perhaps to nurse his injury.

Head down, Cerieda stepped over to the side of the room to wait for a dance that didn't involve any touching.

When one began, she was approached by a dark-haired prince a little older than her. He bowed to her while she curtsied to him, and then they circled each other, both with one arm upraised, their loosely curled hands hovering an inch apart. For the rest of it they danced around each other with hands behind their backs, or gracefully extended their arms in complementary directions. But even so, Cerieda had to keep any eye out and make sure not to accidentally brush up against any of the other dancers. She didn't want the spell to hurt anyone. It gave her a guilty sense of trepidation in the pit of her stomach to feel dangerous in her own skin.

As she and her dance partner headed toward each other again, she realized the next move was for them to link arms. Her breath caught and she missed a step, but her hesitation didn't come soon enough to prevent him from hooking the crooks of their elbows. They swept about in a circle then disengaged, and Cerieda watched him anxiously for signs of the spell taking effect. When several moments passed and nothing adverse seemed to happen to him, she let out a sigh of relief. Maybe arm-in-arm contact didn't count as him touching her, since it wasn't with his hand.

But as soon as the dance was over, Cerieda returned to the sidelines again and stayed there. There was no point risking the welfare of others just for a little fun.

She sat out that part of any of the subsequent balls she was obligated to be present at, too, though everyone started to find her strange for turning down every request, perhaps even thinking she did it because she didn't consider them good enough for her.

Eventually she told her father that he didn't have to keep hosting balls on her account, since odds were that the one whom the spell didn't apply to wasn't likely to be at the next one any more than at the last.

As Cerieda got older, princes and lordlings kept visiting from neighbouring kingdoms and estates to see the beautiful princess, undoubtedly with the goal of establishing a union between their countries or elevating their own status. A few took liberties with a kiss on her hand or a hand on her knee – but shortly thereafter they each suffered unfortunate mishaps, from taking a falling vase to the head to breaking a finger. One princeling once tried to surreptitiously undo the back of her bodice, and somehow managed to cut his finger on her button; another time a lad reached for her derriere, but his hand inexplicably cramped up an inch away from it. Other such attempts were always met with similarly painful or deflective occurrences, and before long the legend of the curse was born.

As it became widespread, the string of suitors dwindled to a stop. The king considered it for the better, since those types clearly weren't in it for the right reasons. Cerieda wasn't so sure. She certainly hadn't appreciated the others trying to take advantage of her, but she didn't want to believe they were all like that. What if these rumours kept away the right one, too?

Chapter 2

Cerieda slowly walked along through the gardens of the palace, gazing down at her hands, folded at her waist. Her twentieth birthday had come and gone, and she was still alone. Many princesses younger than her were already married, or at least in a courtship.

Her peridot-green skirts of silk whispered as she moved. Like the sweet nothings that no one would ever get close enough to whisper in her ear. Aching welled in her heart. She was so lonely. She longed for the touch of a man, to be held and loved, to be able to share with him all the love she had inside. But every prince, every lord, every courtier, every male she ever encountered knew the legend, and avoided her like she was infectious, circumventing a wide space around her whenever they passed. At best they smiled at her and gave a shallow bow, hands tucked safely behind their backs.

She had never been kissed, never held hands, never been romantically embraced, never even been caressed in the slightest. What few suitors she'd had over the years had always stayed a generous distance from her, but since there was no foreseeable advancement to the relationship, they'd all promptly discontinued it.

How was she to know who was meant for her, when no one would risk getting near her? If everyone were to simply give her a tap of the finger, then it would only be a matter of waiting to see who *wasn't* affected by the curse. But they'd never willingly endanger themselves like that – nor did she wish such harm on any of them. Cerieda let out a quiet sigh. Sometimes she wondered if her father had, however inadvertently, condemned her to a life of forlorn solitude.

Cerieda turned down another walkway. The gardens spread extensively behind the north side of the palace, divided into four quarters, with many paths winding through them. She often came out here, where there were fewer people she had to steer clear of – save for the occasional groundskeeper who was there to water the plants or trim the many hedges and topiaries and ornamental saplings. Varnished benches sat at convenient intervals, under a shady tree, in a secluded nook, or facing a particularly scenic view. There was the occasional marble statue of a rearing horse or a swan with uplifted wings, each up on a tall plinth. The elaborate landscaping included all the showiest blooms – coral-pink carnations and sunny daffodils, yellow lilies and white roses and red tulips, all filling the air with their sweet fragrances. It gave her some peace of mind, to just see and smell the flowers – the only things that didn't shy away from her.

Once the afternoon began to turn into evening, Cerieda headed back into the palace. As she proceeded down the hallways of polished stone tiles, she passed several maidservants in simple grey livery. They didn't have to evade her like the men did, but it wasn't their place to get too close to the princess either. She'd occasionally tried to befriend some of the maids who were her age, but they only ever treated her with the respect owed to a superior, not considering themselves her equal. The only other girls she knew were the princesses of other kingdoms, but they only visited a few times a year for social events; not often enough to become close with them.

Cerieda overheard some of the servants gossiping. "...it'll be good to have guests around here again..."

"...I hear the nobleman is quite handsome..."

"Oh, Princess, the king wants to see you," the headmatron remarked to Cerieda as she went by.

With a nod, Cerieda continued to the throne room and turned in through the wide archway. The seat on the low dais ahead wasn't so much a throne as a large chair carved of cherrywood, with inset red upholstery on the seat and back and top of the armrests. The king rarely ever sat in it except on the most official of occasions; he was more often working at his desk off to one side.

Her father spotted her as she came in. "Ah, Cerieda! There you are." He beckoned with an outspread arm. "A nobleman and his scribes arrived today from the northwest kingdom. They'll be staying here for some time while the scribes make copies of several volumes in our library. He graciously offered to have his estate give us rare goods in exchange. It would've been good if you were here to welcome them with me."

She held back a sigh. "Perhaps it's just as well. Being introduced to me might only have driven them away."

The king's face softened with sympathy. "I'm sorry this spell is hard on you. But I did it for your protection."

Cerieda nodded solemnly. "I know, Father."

He gave her a comforting hug, and she put her arms around him too. At least she could still be close with her family. She wondered if he still would've had the spell put on her if it meant he'd never be able to hold his own daughter again either.

The king backed up. "Dinner will be served in about an hour. I'll see you there?"

"Yes. I'll just do some reading until then."

Cerieda went back out into the hall and continued up it until she reached the door to her quarters, on the right. Entering the dimly firelit room, she passed the side of her bed and settled herself in an armchair beside the hearth, curling up with a book of romance. One time, when her father had come upon her reading one such story, he'd expressed concern that it wasn't something he'd necessarily recommend, since it might just make her even more sorely wistful for something she didn't yet have. Which was true, but sometimes it also made her feel better for a while, to vicariously experience the characters falling and being in love, to read about tender kisses and gentle caresses – to become momentarily lost in imagination of another life.

Chapter 3

Cerieda was strolling through the gardens again a few days later. Nearing the point where four walkways met, she lifted her head when she noticed a man coming her way, regarding the flowers. His neat brown hair had a hint of auburn, and he was dressed in a handsome coat befitting a minor nobleman.

He glanced up, and paused when he saw her. "Oh. Good afternoon."

She smiled politely as she came to a stop at the crossroad too. "Afternoon."

"You must be Cerieda. I'm Danavan. I'm having my scribes make copies of some books in the library."

She inclined her head in greeting, but kept her hands folded at her waist. "Welcome to our residence. Forgive me if I don't offer my hand, but I wouldn't want you to be affected by the spell."

His face showed a little concern. "Ah, yes, I've heard."

Cerieda felt like sighing. But she shouldn't be surprised that the word had spread that far, too.

Danavan looked away. "I was heading to see the north garden. Which path were you taking?"

A courteous way to check that their routes didn't overlap. "The same. But I can choose another."

"Oh, no, don't think of it!" he protested. "This is your home – you have the freedom to go where you wish; I'm just the guest here."

Of course; since he was a gentleman, he'd offer to change course himself.

"I'll just accompany you, so long as you don't mind," Danavan finished.

Cerieda flicked her eyes to him at the unexpected suggestion, and cocked her head. "Not at all." They turned and started up the northward walkway. Danavan kept a generous gap between them, his hands clasped behind his back. Cerieda was still considering him. "You're not averse to being near me? Most men make themselves scarce as soon as they hear I'm the one with the curse."

He looked over at her with a quizzically furrowed brow. "Why would I? It's hardly your fault. And I'm sure you have a lovely personality – you deserve companionship as much as anyone else."

Her heart warmed with grateful

appreciation. He was the first man to see it that way. Cerieda turned her head away, watching the stones pass beneath her feet. "Are you liking your stay here?"

"Oh, yes, you have a very splendid home," he replied, admiring the scenery around them. "You should be famous not only for your library, but your gardens as well."

"Did you find all the books you needed there?"

"Even more than I'd hoped for. You have a truly impressive collection. There were several rare volumes I was keen to finally get hold of; *The Workings of Motion and Matter*, *The Explorer's Guide to All the Lands*, *The History of Magic*."

"And why are you looking to copy those? To add to your personal collection?"

"More than that, I intend to make more copies at my estate, then distribute them to other towns and kingdoms. I travel to many places for this same purpose. My goal is to spread knowledge to as many people as possible."

Cerieda studied him with growing admiration. "That's very commendable of you."

Danavan bowed his head. "But I must confess, my interest isn't limited to only the informative texts. I found myself perusing some of the works of fiction here, too. I never can seem to resist re-reading Therion's *Quintessence*."

Her interest sparked up at hearing one of her favourites. " 'For what are we without the ideals that make us strive'," she quoted.

He looked over at her in delight. "You know it, too?"

Cerieda smiled wryly. "Those books have kept me company more often than people."

"Right – you've had access to that library all your life. I wish I could've grown up with such an extensive collection." Danavan gazed off into the distance. "I found it particularly moving when Lucerna throws her mirror into the lake, but the water itself still reflects her face."

"I think it represents letting go of her obsession with how others see her. And in so doing, she discovers her true identity."

His expression was impressed. "That's remarkably insightful."

They arrived at the northern garden, where there were white roses and stone birdbaths and marble statues. They talked for a while more, until a servant came to inform them that the midday meal was about to be served. Danavan walked Cerieda back to the palace. Then, after cordial goodbyes, they parted ways, since the royal family didn't customarily dine with guests on a daily basis.

Over the next while, the two of them came upon each other every now and then, as was to be expected when staying in the same place. Danavan always stopped to say hello, and also engaged her in pleasant conversation whenever they were in each other's company for long, whether they were heading down the same hallway or browsing a shelf in the library or having tea in the parlour. They discussed art and music and literature, statecraft and history and everything in between. It was always a riveting exchange of thoughts and ideas, and they found they shared many perspectives. Cerieda was glad to have someone to talk to – someone who treated her like she was a normal person. Danavan even started coming to see her each day, seemingly for no other reason than to spend longer amounts of time with her. She suspected he might even be asking the servants where she was, to keep finding her so consistently. Of course, there were only so many places she was likely to be.

On one such occasion, he met up with her in the garden and asked if he could join her.

"You have no other business to attend to?" Cerieda teased.

Danavan smiled ruefully. "Well, no, since I've already made my treaty with the king and pointed out the tomes to copy. I'm no scribe; they're the ones who'll do the rest from here, but it could take weeks."

"Then couldn't they do it without you?"

"I could return to my estate, yes, but it wouldn't be right to leave them here unsupervised. I ought to stay and make sure they get the work done. Besides, I'm here to see the sights in this kingdom. That's why I love to travel."

Cerieda settled down onto a bench, and Danavan lowered himself a respectful distance beside her.

"I have to admit, you're rather the main attraction." As she raised her eyebrow at the odd turn of phrase, he went on, "After all those years hearing about the untouchable princess, it's almost like meeting a celebrity."

She smiled bashfully and turned away. "Living under a curse is hardly glamorous."

Danavan studied her intently.

"Have you ever tried to break the spell? There must be some kind of book on the subject."

She looked at him curiously, wondering why he would ask. "My grandfather made it specifically for me. As far as I know, there's never been another one exactly like it before."

"What were the words, exactly? If you don't mind my asking."

Suppressing a trace of abashment, Cerieda repeated them to him. She'd come to memorize it by now, after recalling it dozens of times to make sure she knew how to best avoid inadvertent triggers of it.

Danavan rubbed his chin. "Are there any loopholes? If the suitor were to wear gloves, perhaps?"

She shook her head. "It isn't dependent on direct skin contact. Whether it's through a glove or a sleeve or both, it still takes effect."

"What if it was only a gesture of true friendship? Such as a pat on the back or a hug of congratulations?"

Cerieda smiled sadly. "I've yet to find out. None of the boys I've met seemed interested in being my friend."

There was a trace of sympathy in his eyes. His gaze drifted away, and then he brightened. "How about an act of selfless preservation? Say, if you tripped and he had to catch you? I can't imagine any self-respecting gentleman would be so wary of the curse as to let a lady fall to the ground."

She turned thoughtful. "The spell doesn't say anything about that. But I haven't encountered such a situation, either."

A mischievous smile started

spreading across his face, and she eyed him.

"What?"

Danavan looked away innocently. "I won't suggest an experiment. I doubt it would work the same if it was planned in advance, anyway." He drummed his fingers on his knee. "Has anyone ever bumped into you by accident? Did the curse apply to them, too?"

Cerieda thought back. "That did happen once, years ago, with one of the new servants in the hallway. But nothing consequential seemed to come of it. He considered himself lucky to escape unscathed. The spell mostly has to do with the hands and whether it's done deliberately."

Danavan squinted shrewdly. "What if you were the one who did the touching? Technically, the spell doesn't forbid that."

She eyed him sidelong. "You have a great deal of questions."

He dipped his head sheepishly. "My apologies. I'm just fascinated by your condition."

"Indeed? Most men find it quite the opposite."

Danavan grinned. "Call it my studious nature. And you still haven't answered my question."

Cerieda became introspective. "Well, I've never tried, since I wouldn't want to cause misfortune to them if it didn't work." Her face grew a little warmer, but she continued with the indelicate subject, phrasing it unobtrusively. "Even if I could, it would surely prompt them to reciprocate, and that would still activate the curse. Besides, there's never been anyone I've wanted to get close to." She lowered her eyes. "Much as I wish there was," she added in a whisper. Loneliness welled up in her again as she remembered how she might well always be alone, and she sighed. "Is there something else we could discuss?"

Danavan watched her with commiserative concern. "Of course. I didn't mean to bring up any source of distress."

"I know. It's just that trying to find loopholes made me realize there are none."

"But at least it was fun to speculate for a while there, wasn't it?"

That got a faint smile out of her. It *was* nice to have someone to talk to about it. She couldn't voice her woes to her father, of course, not when he was the one who had sanctioned the spell. And she couldn't discuss loopholes with her grandfather, since he wouldn't want her looking for any in his spell.

Danavan's face became earnest again. "Don't despair, Cerieda. The right man for you is out there somewhere; the spell said so. There's still time."

She looked over at him. Lifting the corner of her mouth in appreciation, she nodded.

Chapter 4

Danavan sat across from Cerieda, playing a game of court at a table in the garden. He wasn't usually so engaged by it, but she was quite a good player.

"What's it like in the northwest kingdom?" she asked conversationally. "Is your estate doing well?"

"Oh, yes, business is good. But to be honest, I'm glad to get a little time away from it." He moved his granite duke piece one square forward, toward her alabaster countess.

She dodged it sideways behind her own jester to prevent him from cornering it. "Something troubling you there?"

Danavan considered his next move. "Well, there are these two farmers on my land," he began. "They've been quarrelling for the longest time. They expect me to resolve it for them, of course. They can't agree on the location of the boundary line between their two fields. Their forefathers founded the farms using a stream to mark the middle of it. But apparently that stream has changed course over the generations, and now it's running through the corner of the second man's farm. The first farmer claims he owns everything up to the western bank, as per the agreement. The other man argues he's entitled to the same amount of land he's always had."

He advanced his earl nearer her baron, but she brought her duchess out from the other side in the direction of his, so he had to whisk his page across two diagonal spaces to come between them.

As Cerieda took her turn again, Danavan went on, "I've considered dividing their properties equally with a fence in the exact middle – but then the first man would no longer have access to the water at all. Or I could officially make the division down the middle of the stream, but then the second farmer would still have the smaller parcel of land." He sighed. "I just don't know what to do about it." He retreated his count behind her herald to avoid being confronted by her marquess.

"Maybe you could divide the land diagonally," Cerieda suggested absently.

He paused, then looked up at her in amazement. "That's brilliant." The farmers would each get half the stream, and yet both their acreage would be the same.

She smiled slightly as she moved her piece. "I learned a few things from my father."

"Well, you're certainly better at mediation than I," Danavan remarked. He waited until her hand was well away from the board before he reached out himself and made his next play.

Cerieda studied the layout for a moment, then took hold of a figure, but hesitated, slowly tapping a slender finger on top of it.

After a minute, he glanced up at her expectantly. "Are you going to make your move?" he prompted.

She met his eyes, a teasing twinkle in her own. "Are you sure you want me to?"

Danavan showed a bit of a smile. "By all means."

She set her emperor down in front

of his prince, thus blocking all his royal pieces with her own and bringing the game to an impasse. He stared at the board, wondering how she'd gotten that past him. Cerieda folded her hands in her lap. "Pardon me for winning. It's in poor taste to best a guest at a game."

But he watched her complacently. "Oh, I hardly mind." It was just another indication of her impressive intellect, and he could hardly hold it against her when she'd just used that same mind to give him an offhand solution to his longstanding problem.

As Danavan was heading to his guest quarters in the palace, he saw the king coming his way. "Your Highness," Danavan greeted smoothly, bowing. He'd exchanged pleasantries in passing with the king before, and even dined with him a few times, and he seemed to find Danavan a likeable guest.

"Ah, Danavan." The king came to a stop before him. "I hear you've been spending time with my daughter." The words gave Danavan a twinge of apprehension in spite of himself. "You're keeping your conduct agreeable, I trust?"

He smiled easily. "Oh, yes, all we do is talk. Cerieda is a scintillating conversationalist. I would never try anything untoward. The spell would surely deter me if I did!"

The king beamed in approval, and clapped him on the shoulder. He was more informal than most kings, but then his was a lesser kingdom than the others. Or perhaps it was because Danavan was only a minor nobleman, not a man of equal rank. "It's good of you to keep her company. There have been so few who were gentlemanly enough to do so."

"It's no trouble at all, I assure you."

The king gave a nod and continued on past him to let him go on his way.

Danavan was walking with Cerieda again through the gardens the next day.

Looking down at the flowers, she tenderly touched a lily petal as she passed, then let her hand trail along the tall grasses. She was so graceful, so beautiful. She had so much gentleness in her, so much love that she wanted to share even with the plants. It was clear why she was considered the fairest princess in the land. Just the sight of her always filled his heart with adoration.

Cerieda paused to bend and take in the aroma of a tulip. When they came near a tree, she went to stand beside it, and put her arms around its trunk like it was a column – or a friend. She tilted the side of her head onto it and smiled at Danavan.

He couldn't help smiling with amusement too. It was a very odd thing to see a princess doing. "You hug a lot of trees?"

"At least they don't mind." She gazed up at the branches. "But it's something I would do, even if it weren't for the spell. Everything deserves to be appreciated."

His admiration for her deepened. It was just like her to have that kind of compassionate outlook. Seeing her soft figure resting against the bole, Danavan almost wished he was the tree.

As the weeks went on, his respect and fondness for her only grew, and he always looked forward to seeing her. She was the highlight of his day. Even when they were apart, he couldn't stop thinking about her, and about her spell, trying to figure out if there was something he could do for her. Then a thought came to him.

The spell only meant she couldn't hug a *person...*

He promptly went to the nearest town and sought out a pedigree dog breeder. Money was no object for Danavan. He bought a silky black shepherd dog and brought him back to the palace.

Danavan came in the back entrance, but stopped in the doorway when the eager dog tugged forward to the end of his leash. Danavan had to maintain a hold on it to keep him in check.

Cerieda was coming up the hall toward them. "Who is this?" she greeted in delight, kneeling to smooth a hand over the dog's head. He nosed at her cheek, tail wagging so enthusiastically his whole body waggled.

"His name is Midnight. He's for you," Danavan said, and Cerieda looked up at him in wonder. "I figured, at least with him, you could have a companion with whom you can share affection freely."

Bowing her head, she looked into the dog's eyes, tousling her hands over his fur. "You are so *sweet*," she cooed.

Danavan slid his hands into his pockets. "The breeder assures me that he's the friendliest, quietest purebred in the kennel."

She glanced up at Danavan with a small smile. "I didn't mean the dog," she murmured warmly.

His mouth slowly spread into a smile too.

Cerieda kept stroking Midnight, and even wrapped her arms around his neck in a hug.

Danavan smiled wider. It did his heart good to see her expressing her warmth without inhibition. *And then whenever you're with him, you'll think of me.*

The king came in from an archway, and paused when he saw the dog. "What's this?" There was clear disapproval in his tone. He glanced at Danavan, then back to Midnight. "Such a rambunctious playmate is hardly fit for a princess," he objected.

Dismay tweaked Danavan. He hadn't considered whether the king would oppose it.

"Oh, Father, please let me keep him," Cerieda pleaded. "It would mean so much to me."

The king watched her hugging the dog for a moment; then his face softened into an indulgent smile. "Very well. Anything for you, Cerieda." She beamed with gratitude. "But he'll have to be housed in the servants' quarters. I don't want him running loose in the palace."

"Of course." Cerieda got up and started heading down the hall, still looking over her shoulder at Midnight. She patted a hand on the side of her skirt. "Come on, Midnight!" she invited, and the dog readily bounded along beside her.

Smiling, Danavan turned down a side passage.

Chapter 5

Danavan strolled alongside Cerieda through the summer air of the gardens. He'd been there almost a month, though it seemed like it'd gone by all too soon.

"So, how are the scribes coming along?" she prompted. "Are they just about done?" She sounded almost like she'd be disappointed if that was the case.

He kept his voice casual. "Yes, but I assigned them a few more, smaller books. I figured I might as well get some of my favourites down while we're here." He proffered a smile. In actuality, he'd done it just so he would have a reason to remain that much longer.

Cerieda seemed to brighten a little. "Oh." Her tone was more hopeful. They settled onto a bench. "I think this is a record for how long I've known someone since the spell was enacted," she remarked lightly.

Danavan started mustering his courage. "I have to say, I admire your fortitude, living with the spell without even becoming bitter about it. I can't imagine what it must be like."

Cerieda lowered her eyes. "It hasn't been easy. But I've made my peace with it."

He wanted so much to comfort her, to put an arm around her shoulders, or just to show her how he felt about her. But he couldn't. Danavan turned his face away, and saw a yellow lily that stood beside his knee. He picked it, intending to gift it to Cerieda. But then he had a thought. Holding it by the end of the stem, he lowered it so the flowerhead trailed across the back of her hand. Cerieda looked at it, then lifted her eyes to him. No harm came to him, since it didn't count as him touching her. Lifting the flower, Danavan stroked its soft petals along her cheek in lieu of a tender hand. "Look at that, I found a loophole," he murmured.

Her eyes softened, and a trace of pink rose to her cheeks. But she didn't move away. He offered her the lily, and she accepted it gingerly, careful not to let her fingers brush his while taking hold of the stem. Cerieda bowed her head over it, inhaling its scent. It was such a feminine pose.

A wavy lock of hair slid down by her cheek, making the image even more perfect. And yet he felt an urge to tuck it back for her.

Danavan folded his elbow up on the back of the bench. "Does hair qualify as part of the spell?" he whispered.

Cerieda turned her head slightly to eye him past the kiss curl. "It might not," she admitted, sounding curious to find out.

The amplitude of his emotions made him daring. Very carefully, he reached a hand out, well above her shoulder, and took the end of the strand between his first two fingers. Cerieda stayed still, watching him. When there was no repercussion, not even so much as a static shock, he drew the strand back and looped it behind her ear. Then, unable to resist, he sank his hand into the back of her thick golden hair, gently closing his fingers around it, without getting near her neck. Her tresses were soft and warm and smooth. It had him breathing deeply, just to hold a part of her, however innocuous – to have his hand that much closer to her face.

His heart was so full. Even this brief contact nearly made it overflow. Danavan slowly withdrew his arm and clasped his hands together, before he could be tempted to do more.

"How's Midnight doing?" he asked, still softly.

Cerieda gave him a warm smile. "He's a dear. I can't thank you enough. It's the most considerate thing anyone's done for me." Still meeting his eyes, she traced a finger along the edge of one of the lily petals. "And I want you to know, I'm grateful for all the time you've spent with me. I've never had so good a friend as you."

Danavan slowly smiled, and nodded a little. But even at the same time as his heart was warmed by her sentiment, there was a trace of resignation in the pit of his stomach. She, in her innocence, probably saw him as nothing more than a friend. And why wouldn't she, when he was nothing special, and she deserved so much better? He shouldn't compromise that by implying he had deeper feelings for her than that. Besides, what hope did he have? He couldn't truly act on it anyway, not with the curse.

Late that night, Danavan took a walk in the empty hallways, deep in thought. *What am I to do?* He was in love with Cerieda – there was no mistaking it. But he could never actually touch her. *Leave it to me and my romantic folly to fall for the only girl in the land who's utterly off-limits.* They had no future together. How could they, when he would never be able to fully express his affection for her, not even with a hug or a hand on hers? Their relationship could never be more than it was now: being in each other's company, talking, engaging in pastimes together – but always an inch apart.

Furthermore, he couldn't stay here in the palace forever. He'd already extended his visit longer than he'd planned. He would have to be leaving soon. And then he wouldn't even get to see her anymore. *Should I tell her how I feel before I leave?* Danavan ruminated on that, but ultimately decided against it, with some dejection. It would probably just cause her unnecessary distress.

But if he did let her know, could he chance one intimate moment with her before he went out of her life? Or if he stayed, was there any way to make it work? Would it be worth suffering a few injuries, if it meant he'd get to hold her, to kiss her? The more liberties he took, the worse the repercussions might be. But if they only happened once after each act, perhaps he could just recover in between, as long as it wasn't too severe.

But no. If she didn't feel the same, he would never try to take it further. He would just have to cherish what time he had left with her, then go back to his kingdom and hope that, somehow, time and distance would dilute his memory of her and lessen his heartbreak.

A stifling tension banded his chest. His desperation to hold back the anguish made it seem hard to breathe. He felt trapped amidst heat and aggravation, even while stubborn resistance churned within him. He didn't want to stop loving her. He didn't think he could. Why should he have to, when she was so deserving of love, when sharing that love with her was supposed to be a good thing?

He surely wasn't the first man to fall for her. With her kind green eyes, her gentle nature, all of her shaped and proportioned perfectly... But there was no reason to think that such an exceptional woman as her would love an ordinary man like him.

As Danavan neared the royal wing, he noticed that the door to Cerieda's chambers stood ajar. He drifted to a stop outside it. Torchlight spilled into the room, dimly illuminating Cerieda's blanketed form. Affection welled in him. He slipped in, just to look upon her for a moment. She lay asleep in the silken sheets of her luxurious bed, her head partly turned away. Danavan softly stepped closer, and knelt by her side.

Her golden tresses fanned out on the pillow around her head like the rays of the rising sun. Her hair smelled like daffodils in the morning light. Danavan leaned forward, extending a hand toward her sweet face. He paused a hair's breadth from her cheek, yearning so much to touch that smooth, fair skin. But he hesitated, sighing inwardly, knowing well the consequences.

Cerieda stirred ever so slightly, turning her head so that his suspended fingers brushed her cheek. Danavan withdrew his hand with a silent gasp, and looked at it in wonder. A thrill of hope rose in his heart, but it was soon replaced by wariness as he stood, glancing about the dark room, then went back out the door.

From then on he went around

tense and alert for signs of his impending doom, eyeing every gardener with a pair of shears that might trip toward him, on the lookout for any brick that might come loose and catch him on the head. He also avoided Cerieda with a will, lest he accidentally come into contact with her again and worsen his fate. But the days went on, and nothing terrible befell him, nothing at all out of the ordinary – not so much as a stubbed toe.

At last Danavan slowed down and began to wonder – could this mean...he was the one man who was exempt from the curse? The one she truly loved, as much as he loved her – the only one she could ever be with?

Surely that was too much to hope. Maybe it just didn't count as an infraction, because he hadn't been the one to initiate the touch.

But if there was any chance for him, he couldn't give up until he found out for sure – even if it meant risking a little injury.

Chapter 6

Cerieda paced along the corridor, a trace of worry in her heart. Danavan hadn't come to see her in days. A few times, she thought she'd even glimpsed him just before he dodged out of sight, as if he was deliberately avoiding her. *Have I finally scared him off?* She didn't want to lose his friendship, even if they could never be more than that. She didn't think she could bear it if the only man she'd gotten close to were to shut her out too.

She knew Danavan would have to return to his own kingdom before long. But Cerieda was hoping that perhaps they could at least exchange correspondences by letter after that, and still continue their association that way. She hadn't yet suggested it to him, since she didn't want to seem presumptuous.

She was missing him already, even after so short a time apart. She'd enjoyed every minute they were together. He was so ingenious, finding little ways around her spell, ones that even she hadn't been looking for. No other man had cared enough to bother. Buying her a dog she could hug, stroking her with a flower... She remembered how it had trailed tingles across her skin. And when he'd touched her hair...it had been such an intimate moment. She welcomed the gesture when it came from Danavan. Her heart filled with warmth just thinking about him. She'd never felt this for anyone else before. She couldn't imagine going back to a life without him.

What if she was falling for him even when he wasn't the one the spell referred to? Was that even possible? Could they be doomed to be tragic lovers who could never be together? That would be too cruel.

At last, she spotted Danavan in the hall ahead, walking slowly with his back to her.

"Danavan," she greeted softly as she came up behind him, and he turned abruptly, sidestepping so he was out of the way. "I haven't seen you in a while," she went on with some concern. "Is everything all right?"

He looked glad to see her. "There's something I want to test. It might be a risk, but I don't care at this point." He reached for her hand, but she reflexively lifted it back.

"What...?" she breathed, aghast. "You shouldn't – you know what will happen." She very much didn't want him to get hurt because of her curse.

Danavan gave her a slight smile. "Bear with me. I don't think it will." And he gently took her hand in his own. Cerieda drew in a breath. He stroked his other hand atop hers, surrounding it in his warm hold. His hands were so manly, yet cradled hers with such caring.

She looked at their hands in wonder. No dire result was afflicting Danavan. "How can it be...?"

"How I've longed to tell you. I'm in love with you, Cerieda. Deeply and truly."

Her heart skipped a beat, and she lifted her gaze to his. It was more than she could've hoped for. She was filled with such affection and gratitude that her eyes almost misted up. "Oh, Danavan," she whispered. "You're my first and only love."

Relieved adoration came over his face. He tenderly set his hand on her cheek, and Cerieda felt a surge of sweet yearning to finally be touched like that. Squeezing her eyes closed, she leaned into his palm. It was all so overwhelming. Danavan was the exception to the spell after all! She was so indescribably glad it was him, and not someone else.

Cerieda gazed up at him again. Danavan lightly ran his hand down her arm to hold her other hand in his. "You'll never have to be alone again," he said softly.

Warmth rose to her cheeks. She dearly appreciated his words. "You'll stay?"

Danavan smiled. "Of course. Even magic spells couldn't keep me away."

Cerieda grinned. "I'm so happy it turned out to be you. We must tell my family!" she enthused. She turned and hastened down the hallway along with him, holding her skirt clear with one hand as she headed to the throne room.

"Father, look!" she called as she hurried in, and the king glanced up. "I've found the one the spell spoke of! It's Danavan!" As they came to a stop, she held Danavan's hand in hers, linking fingers with it and lifting it up for her father to see. Danavan watched her with a contented expression.

The king looked from one to the other, but when the curse didn't take effect, his face bloomed into a beam. "This is phenomenal!" he exclaimed, spreading his arms as he came over to them. Cerieda's grandfather drifted in the archway at the back corner of the room, likely to investigate the commotion. The king looked over his shoulder at him, and beckoned. "Come see! Is this really the right one?"

Studying Danavan, the shaman crossed to them, his staff clicking on the floor. He was thin and slightly stooped under his robes, with a wiry grey beard and long hair below his bald pate. When he arrived before Danavan and Cerieda, he wove his staff over their heads, squinting searchingly. "The spell is still in place. It will continue to apply to everyone else. But it has indeed recognized him as the only one who was ever meant to be exempt from it." He smiled too.

Cerieda and Danavan shared an exuberant glance.

"Well, I'll be!" the king remarked. "And he was right here all this time!" Then he eyed Danavan closely, and lowered his voice. "Just because you *can* do anything with her now, I hope it doesn't mean you *have...?*"

"Oh, no, Father, we only just found out!" Cerieda dismissed lightly.

The king studied both of them for a moment, then nodded, his expression clearing. He turned his attention back to Danavan. "Well, Danavan, now that you know, what do you intend to do next?"

Danavan looked over at Cerieda with tender eyes and a warm smile. "Marry her, of course," he murmured.

A soft gasp escaped her, and she gazed at him in delight.

"That is, if you'll have me," he added. "Forgive me, I meant to ask you more formally."

"Oh, of course I'll marry you!" Cerieda breathed, turning to him and taking hold of his other hand too.

The king set a hand on each of their backs. "Then I can have no objections. Will you be wanting to hold the wedding here in the palace?"

Cerieda brightened. "That would be great." She looked at Danavan to check with him.

"Sounds good to me," he agreed, then promptly turned and towed her out the archway. "Let's go pick out which room to use!"

She was in just as much of a breathless whirl as he, but she managed to hang back on his hand to pause him in the hallway. "But wait, we should take a moment to plan first, since we're about to spend our life together!" Danavan turned back to her with a twinkle in his eye. "Where shall we live?" It was customary for the man to whisk his bride off to his land, but in this case Cerieda was the one with the higher royal status, so she could hardly leave the kingdom she might have to rule one day. Besides, she didn't think her father would appreciate it, either.

Danavan considered her, then smiled. "I wouldn't want to steal you away from the palace, especially when my manor isn't nearly as grand. But perhaps it'd still be better for us to have a home of our own. I'm sure there's some lovely mansion near here that we can settle into."

Cerieda beamed. "I think I know just the place." Then she became earnest with some concern. "But what of your estate?"

"Oh, I can have my steward manage things there. And maybe I'll visit from time to time to check in on the place, for a change of scenery." Danavan smiled wider. "In fact, I'd like for you to see it sometime."

Chapter 7

Cerieda and Danavan stopped by different parts of the palace, looking around in first the parlour then the gardens, and settled on the grand hall for the location of the ceremony.

That afternoon, they took a carriage to see the mansion Cerieda had in mind. It was just five hours away to the northwest, halfway between the palace and Danavan's kingdom. It was owned by her cousin, but she only frequented it in the summer. She was there at the time, and they discussed the possibility with her while taking a tour of the sunny interior and grounds, which they both thought would be perfect for them. Since Cerieda's cousin was an incurable romantic, she readily agreed to the idea of offering them a marital home as a wedding gift.

They returned to the palace, and the next day, they met with the king again in the throne room, where he was conferring with his advisor and Cerieda's grandfather. They told the king of their plans and that they were ready to get married at the soonest opportunity.

"Don't you feel you're perhaps rushing into this?" the king put forward.

"Why wait?" Cerieda countered blithely. "The spell proves we're meant for each other. We've already known each other for a month."

"And we're quite in love," Danavan added warmly, and she smiled broadly at him in agreement.

"And my closest family is right here." She paused. "Oh. Although, wouldn't you want your own family to attend, Danavan?"

He glanced up in abrupt recollection. "Ah, yes, I suppose it would be good if they were here to see it. I can just send them invitations, while the other preparations are underway." He gave her a brief beam. "It won't take them long to arrive."

"Who will officiate?" the advisor prompted.

The king looked at Cerieda. "Why not your grandfather?" he suggested. "As a shaman, he's qualified to serve in that capacity."

She nodded thoughtfully. "It would be nice to keep it in the family." But then she eyed her grandfather shrewdly. "As long as you don't try to slip any more spells in there," she warned playfully.

He showed a bit of an impish smile. "Are you sure? I could easily whip up a complementary one for Danavan that deters women. You'd make a matching couple."

"Oh, Grandfather, don't even suggest!" Cerieda protested with a laugh.

"It won't be needed, anyway," Danavan put in, smiling gently over at Cerieda. "You're the only woman for me."

Her heart warmed, and she lowered her eyes with bashful pleasure.

Danavan sent his scribes back to his estate with the copied books and letters to be delivered by courier from there to his family. Cerieda's father invited distant relatives, as well as dignitaries from all across the land, including the princes and lords that had once attempted to court her, so as to show everyone that the spell had worked. The king also took it upon himself to arrange every detail of the ceremony, sparing no expense to make it as lavish an event for Cerieda as could be.

Other than being consulted on a few decisions, such as what bridal dress she wanted made, she and Danavan mostly had the time to themselves. Cerieda did notice the chamberlain always keeping an eye on the two of them, to make sure they were never alone together for too long; undoubtedly by her father's request. But it wasn't called for; they never did much more than hold hands.

Sometimes, when they stood looking into each other's eyes in a secluded hallway, Danavan would stroke a gentle hand on her shoulder...or her elbow...or the side of her neck, acclimatizing her to his touch, little by little. Every caress let her feel how much he loved her, and made her adore him all the more.

The most it led up to was when Danavan enfolded her in an embrace, and she looped her arms about his neck. He drew her closer by the waist like he never wanted to let go, nestling his head beside hers. Being in a hug with Danavan was entirely different experience. It made her warm all over. With their hearts right near each other, it filled hers with devoted contentment.

Finally, the week of waiting passed, and the wedding took place in the grand hall, which was festooned with golden draperies and dozens of glowing candelabras. The guests sat on benches that had been brought in for the purpose, facing where Cerieda stood with Danavan before her grandfather. Midnight even sat at the front, upon Cerieda's insistence. A servant boy had his arm around the silky dog's back to keep him there.

Her grandfather began speaking. "Today we are gathered here to celebrate the happiness that these two people have found. The spell placed on Princess Cerieda was designed to thwart any man who is not her true love. It has proven its worth twofold, for now it has verified the identity of the one who was always meant for her. This union is attended by magic, for there is none more powerful than true love."

Danavan and Cerieda turned to each other. She had her hands folded before her skirt; his were clasped behind his back. Danavan didn't take his eyes off hers.

The shaman went on, "Danavan, since you wish to become Cerieda's husband, you will be obliged to love her and only her, to support and respect her, for all your life. Will you take this vow as your own?"

Danavan's gaze was full of love. "I will."

"Cerieda, since you wish to become Danavan's wife, you will be obliged to love him and only him, to support and respect him, for all your life. Will you take this vow as your own?"

She could scarcely contain her ebullience. It was hard to believe it had only been a month ago that she'd thought she'd never find love, and now she was about to be married to Danavan. "I will."

"Then, with my power as a shaman, in the presence of magic, the king, and your kinfolk, I declare that the two of you are hereupon united in matrimony. You may now kiss the princess."

Danavan gently set his hands on either side of Cerieda's face, stroking his thumbs there, and gave her a small smile. Her cheeks grew warmer at his touch, and her heart started beating faster in anticipation. Then Danavan slowly leaned in, tilting his head, and tenderly kissed her. Cerieda inhaled with the sweet thrill that rose in her. Her lips tingled; it felt so foreign, but so gratifying, to have his face so close, his lips surrounding hers. She absently rested light hands on his chest.

When Danavan backed away to meet her eyes again, Cerieda's heart leapt at the realization they were officially married. It was a great comfort to know they'd have a lifetime to hold each other. And Cerieda quivered with excitement to think that after tonight, there wasn't a single part of her that would remain untouched.

Island in the Sky

~ Prologue ~

The Ramseys walked along the sunlit path that led through the uncultivated fields to town. Mr. Ramsey, a tall fellow with a wiry frame despite all his years felling trees, held one of the mule's reins as he kept pace alongside it with his wife. The simple lorry the mule pulled had no driver's bench, only a flat cartbed to carry all the long planks of lumber to be sold at the market.

Mrs. Ramsey thought she heard a faint giggling despite the trundle of the wheels. She turned her head toward the meadow on the right, where it had seemed to come from. "Did you hear that?" she asked her husband, who blankly followed her gaze. The sound came more distinctly this time, and she put a hand in front of Mr. Ramsey's chest. "Shh!" He obligingly brought the rumbling cart to a stop, and they listened for a moment. Into the silence rose another bout of baby-like laughter and cooing. "It sounds like a child," she breathed, and headed off in the direction of it. Hesitating, Mr. Ramsey looked around, then led the mule over to a shrubby tree and tied the reins to a branch before trailing after his wife.

Mrs. Ramsey drew up short at what she saw. A blonde girl, little more than a year old, sat amidst the tall grass, giggling in delight as she batted at the stalks with her little hand. She wore a pretty sky-blue dress with gathered capsleeves. A yellow-and-black butterfly fluttered past her face, and her eyes latched onto it. She cooed, reaching out for it.

Mrs. Ramsey stared at her in bewilderment. "How did you get all the way out here?" She looked out over the landscape, scanning all around for where the girl's family might be, but there was no one in sight. What kind of people would leave a toddler in the middle of nowhere? *And how long has it been since she ate*? Mrs. Ramsey stooped and lifted the girl up into her arms.

"Don't go jus' pickin' up a strange child," Mr. Ramsey protested.

"We can't just leave her here," she countered. It was her natural motherly instinct to get the wee thing off the ground and keep her safe. Besides, the tot didn't seem to mind; she looked perfectly content, simply putting her knuckles in her mouth.

Mrs. Ramsey noticed the sparkle of a silver necklace at the babe's neck, and lifted its fine chain, on which hung a set of carved letters that spelled out a name. "Celeste," she read. She didn't know of anybody around here who could afford such pricy jewelry for their children. She hadn't seen anyone with quite so bonnie a baby, either. "Let's see if anyone in town is missing her."

They returned to the path and continued on for another hour until they reached the village. On their way to the market, they asked everyone they saw if Celeste was theirs or if they knew of anyone who had lost track of their toddler, but all they got were shaken heads and quizzical looks. While Mr. Ramsey bartered with the timber merchant, Mrs. Ramsey kept asking around nearby. She also bought Celeste a soft cookie treat, to make sure she didn't go hungry. Once the sale of the wood was made, they even went around knocking on doors, though the few who did answer often found the intrusion irritating or were indignant at the accusation that they'd misplace their own child. Finally, the Ramseys drifted back into the square, with no choice but to conclude that Celeste's family wasn't in this town. But the next closest settlements were miles away, too far for a tot to have wandered from. And the Ramseys couldn't go and check them all. Hopefully word of their little search would spread to whomever she did belong to, whether it was someone they missed here or elsewhere.

Mrs. Ramsey sighed. "Well, looks like no one here will claim the poor thing." She looked down at Celeste with indecision. "Maybe...we should keep her."

Mr. Ramsey's straggly eyebrows went up. "We can't afford another mouth to feed. We've a hard enough time keeping ourselves fed."

"We've been putting some money away."

"That's fer retirement! I won't be able to keep choppin' wood ferever! Besides, we're too old to be raisin' another youngun from scratch."

"Oh, nonsense. I'm not yet fifty, and you don't have many years on me. We can handle a little darling like her." She touched a tender finger onto the tip of the girl's nose. "I always wanted a daughter."

"What use have we for a girl? She won't be cut out fer labour like sons are."

"We already had four of those. Good-for-nothin's. They all off workin' their own crafts and farms, with never a thought for how we're getting by."

"That's jus' 'cause lumberjackin' ain't a trade as can be passed on. They jus' tryin' to make more prosperous lives fer themselves."

"Well, knowin' them, they won't be wantin' another baby neither, not when they got more of their own on the way. We're all this child has."

"I still say it's none of our business," Mr. Ramsey muttered. He watched Celeste for a quiet moment as she sucked on her necklace, looking up at them with big green eyes. "She is a precious t'ing, though," he murmured, and stroked a gentle hand on her blonde head. Then he set a fist on his hip and scowled. "Awright, we'll take her in," he declared grudgingly, and Mrs. Ramsey beamed. "But she's goin' back at the first sign of her parents comin' to get her!"

"Absolutely!" Hiking the tot closer, Mrs. Ramsey started off for home, her grumbling husband trailing behind with the mule cart.

~ Chapter 1 ~

Celeste gazed up at the distant island, suspended high in the blue sky. She often came here to look at it. And to wonder what it was like up there. She'd heard tales of it ever since she was a little girl, even in the far southwest, and it had always fascinated her. A few globular white clouds floated near the horizon and around the isle, not much higher than it. A gull coasted along through the air, then landed on the grassy brink of the island. It was so odd that they had a perch higher than any tree rising from the ground. It wasn't a very large parcel of land, but it was still visible for miles around. Tourists came from all over to visit the single most extraordinary phenomenon in the world. In fact, Celeste caught a glint of sunlight off a shuttlecraft that was slowly heading there now, to convey its load of passengers. But her family had never been able to afford the fare.

The tall grasses around her swayed in the breeze, brushing against the skirt of her light-blue dress. She absently stroked her hand over their tips. A stronger gust tossed her wavy blonde hair about, and she sighed, pushing it back with her hands. *I'd better get back home.* She turned to walk back through the bright yellow-green field.

It was a long way back to the house, and by the time she got there, the island was little more than a faraway dot behind her. Green fields of rye surrounded the modest farmhouse of faded wooden boards. One of Mrs. Ramsey's sons had let his mother and Celeste stay here in an extra building on the far side of his farm. They'd moved here five years ago, after Mr. Ramsey passed. Celeste still missed him and his simple gentleness sometimes. In his later years, when he was too old to keep logging, he'd taken up carving, which had always been a hobby. But there wasn't much of a market for whimsical owl sculptures, and it wasn't as lucrative as the timber trade even when there were buyers. Their funds had dwindled, and after he was gone, they'd had no source of income at all. There were always plenty of strong young men coming from town to cut down trees in the forest they lived near, and they weren't about to share any of the profits with the Ramsey women. They couldn't afford to keep living there, so they'd had no choice but to leave the house and stay with one of Mrs. Ramsey's sons in the area. But each of them had their hands full with their own teeming families and demanding work, and didn't have spare room or money to accommodate them for long. Then, finally, they'd gotten a letter back from her farmer son in the midland, who was slightly more well-off and had a spare house available for them. Celeste still thought of him as Mrs. Ramsey's son, not really her own brother, though she'd always called the Ramseys Mother and Father.

She'd known from the beginning that she was a foundling. But where she came from was an unsolvable mystery; all the Ramseys knew was that her name was Celeste, from her necklace. She was grateful that they hadn't kept the knowledge from her, but as a result, she'd always felt a bit distanced from her family, different than the other children who were raised by their birth parents. It didn't help that the Ramsey boys hadn't spent much time with her when they did visit, and the one they were living with now hadn't even met her before she got there.

When Celeste stepped in the door, she heard talking in the kitchen ahead.

"You know I'm fine with boarding you here, but that Celeste is another matter." It was the voice of Mrs. Ramsey's son. "The least she could do is help you out around the house more. But she's too dignified for that, of course."

Celeste drifted across the dim sitting room toward the archway.

"She does help. She keeps me company when no one else does." Mrs. Ramsey's tone was rather pointed.

"Where is she now, then? She's always off staring at that island, wasting time with her head up in the clouds. She's a grown woman – she should be married by now, or at least looking for a husband among the many young men in the towns around here. Then she'd be his responsibility."

Celeste came near enough to see into the other room. Mrs. Ramsey, a stocky but weathered woman, stood on the other side of the kitchen table facing her son. Her grey hair, streaked with a few white strands, was rolled at the nape of her neck as usual. She squared her shoulders in response to her son's comment. "She'll get married when she's good an' ready! If it's not somethin' she wants to do yet, I ain't gonna force her to!"

Her eyes flicked to Celeste as she came in, and Farmer Ramsey turned his head to glance at Celeste too. He was in his forties, and his own children were nearly Celeste's age, so it was little wonder he couldn't quite see her as a sister.

"Don't argue on account of me,"

Celeste said quietly. She never wanted there to be conflict. She'd even mediated little disagreements between Mr. and Mrs. Ramsey when she was younger. It was harder to do when she was the subject of the dispute.

Farmer Ramsey brushed past Celeste on his way out. "See you later."

Celeste continued closer to Mrs. Ramsey. "Maybe I *should* think of something to profit the family."

Mrs. Ramsey gave her a slight smile. "Don't let him get to you. He's just worried about the income from his crops this year."

Celeste sighed. "I wish Father was here."

Mrs. Ramsey wrapped a comforting arm around her shoulders. "I know. As do I."

~ Chapter 2 ~

Celeste came downstairs the next morning and went into the sunlit kitchen to prepare some breakfast for herself and Mrs. Ramsey. She heard the front door creak open and closed, and then Mrs. Ramsey came shuffling in, looking through a handful of letters.

Her steps halted abruptly. "Oh, Celeste, look what came in the mail for you today! It says you've won a trip to the Floating Island!" She handed Celeste a shimmering golden ticket.

Her heart leapt as she took it. "What? But I haven't entered a lottery..." She looked down at it.

CELESTE RAMSEY,

YOU'VE BEEN RANDOMLY SELECTED
AS 1 OF 100 LUCKY WINNERS OF
A FREE DAY TRIP TO THE FLOATING ISLAND!

PRESENT THIS TICKET AT THE SHUTTLE STATION WITHIN THE NEXT 2 WEEKS AND ENJOY YOUR VISIT!

She could hardly believe it. She glanced up. "May I, Mother?"

"Of course! I know how much you've always wanted to go."

"But I'll still have to get there somehow..." It would be too far to walk.

Mrs. Ramsey thought for a minute. Then she lifted a finger. "Oh! I think one of the neighbouring farmers is going to be cartin' another batch of supplies to the island – in just a few days' time, if I'm not mistaken. I'm sure he wouldn't mind giving you a lift."

"But he won't be staying there for hours, will he? How will I get back?"

Mrs. Ramsey paused. "Maybe you can hitch a ride back with some other tourists headed this way. I'll give you a few of my spare coins in case you need to pay fer transport for yourself. If nothin' else, I'll borrow my son's draft horse and come get you myself."

Celeste smiled in appreciation. She was grateful that at least Mrs. Ramsey still had her back.

"I'll go check with the neighbour this afternoon," Mrs. Ramsey added.

Celeste could hardly contain her

expectancy for the few hours until Mrs. Ramsey set out to the adjacent farm, and had an even harder time waiting for her to get back. When she finally returned, it was all Celeste could do to keep from bobbing on her toes as Mrs. Ramsey hung up her shawl on the wall peg beside the front door before she began speaking.

"Don't look so anxious, Celeste! The farmer says it's fine."

Celeste clasped her hands in delight.

"It's three days from now. But he'll be headin' out at first light, so you'll have to be ready by then."

That was fine by Celeste; it just meant all the more hours of daylight she could spend on the island.

Celeste got up at dawn on the designated day, and put on her best dress – a simple, draping, floor-length gown of dusky grey, with a soft collar and long, slightly flared sleeves. She slid her golden ticket into a flat pocket sewn onto the hip of the skirt, along with the five coppers Mrs. Ramsey had given her. She didn't pack anything else, since she would be back home in time for supper.

She gave Mrs. Ramsey a goodbye kiss on the cheek on her way out and hastened through the dim fields to meet the neighbour at his farm. She climbed up onto the cartbench beside the wizened old man, who then flapped the reins to start his weary nag plodding.

After a while of silence, the farmer made an attempt at conversation. "So, I hear you won a tour of the island. That's some trip."

Celeste turned to him avidly. "Have you ever been?"

"Oh, gracious, no. I'm not terribly fond of heights. I don't see what all the fuss is about, livin' on a chunk of land way up in the air, all precarious-like. I much prefer the good ol' solid ground, meself."

Celeste looked away, suppressing a bit of a smile. He reminded her a little of Mr. Ramsey. He'd always been the down-to-earth sort, too.

She lifted her eyes to the faraway island, and watched it slowly grow closer as the hours dragged on.

***

The captain stood with fists on his hips, watching his men heft the canister down from the covered wagon onto the ground before him. He ran his hand down the smooth steel. The cylinder stood as high as a man, with many airtight seams and interlocking mechanisms, as well as a smaller, sealed pipe rising from the top. He'd found it deep within a cave while looting the stash of another pirate. Legend said it would unleash a terrible power that could take control of others. And the captain reckoned that if he was the one to release it, command of that power would be his, like letting a djinn out of a bottle.

But it could only be opened at an altitude higher than seven thousand feet. Even if there were a mountain nearby, it would be too laborious to climb it and lug the canister along with them. He only knew of one place that was that far up. He turned to look out from the small stand of trees they stood in, at the sky-island in the distance. The Floating Land.

He lowered his eyes to the shuttle station below it. All they would have to do was wait for one of the shuttles to empty of tourists, then slip aboard behind cover of the crowd and fly it to the island after picking up the canister from the copse. It should be doable without attracting attention. But if someone *did* get in their way... The captain pushed back his long red coat to rest his hand on the wood handle of his iron pistol, and smirked. He'd have to do some convincing.

~ Chapter 3 ~

The farmer pulled his cart up. "This is my stop," he told Celeste. She thanked him for the lift and stepped down off the side of the wagon bench. The island loomed high in the sky overhead. She'd never been this close to it. The shuttle station was still well outside its shadow, which lay some distance further ahead.

A large crowd milled around the

station. As Celeste became caught up in the eddying tide of people, an official directed her and the others with an arm held out. "Incomers this way. Single file."

The tourists ahead of her formed a line, and soon Celeste could see they were being herded down a lane that led beside a small ticket booth. There were several more in a row to either side. Beyond this one, a shuttle rested atop four thick supports standing several feet high, a section of its side lowered to make a ramp reaching the ground. The shuttle was made of silvery-grey metal panels, with a slanted, tinted windshield wrapping partway around, and a high window across the length of each side.

As they came up, the previous batch of tourists were disembarking from another shuttle on the left. Celeste arrived in time to see the last one lift a necklace off over his head, depositing it in the small opening of a varnished wooden box on the counter.

The person ahead of her finished paying the fellow manning the admissions booth, and the rest of the queue proceeded closer to the waiting shuttle.

When Celeste got to the booth, she brought out her golden ticket for the man to see, and he nodded, letting her keep it. But before she got on the shuttle, she had to sign a waiver providing her first and last name and next of kin, releasing the inhabitants of the Floating Land from liability in the event of the undersigned suffering from altitude sickness, falling off the edge of the island, or any number of other unfortunate eventualities. Celeste felt a bit of trepidation, but swallowed and signed the paper. She'd come too far to turn back now. Besides, things like that hardly ever happened anyway; they just had to list all the remote possibilities to cover their bases.

Then it was her turn to approach the shuttle and walk up the entry ramp into it.

The interior was big enough for about twenty people, with a row of upholstered grey benches on either side of a wide aisle. Celeste went to take an unoccupied seat on the right. Once the rest of the places had been filled by tourists, the hatch slowly lifted and closed. It was quieter and dimmer inside now, and strips of white crystal glowed along the floor to mark the sides of the aisle.

A female attendant stepped out of a door at the front of the shuttle, where a compartment was sectioned off for the pilot. "Please remain seated for the duration of the ride," she said to the passengers in a cool voice. "Liftoff will now commence. We will arrive at the island in a few minutes." Then she went back in.

The shuttle started sluggishly, lifting off the struts and turning to ascend gradually toward the island. Celeste felt a sort of giddy suspense in her middle. She looked out the window beside her, watching the ground shrink away, until the haze of an interposing cloud obscured it from view. Then she craned her neck to look forward out of the glass.

A few wisps of cloud passed over the shuttle's nose, and then they broke out into a spectacular panorama. They were amidst a field of clouds, slowly rising between towering masses of bright white domes with shadowed underbellies. They were even more beautiful and immense from here. It took her breath away to be above the clouds.

For as long as she could remember, she'd always had dreams of clouds. This was almost like that - except, of course, in the dream, she'd been gliding among them without a shuttle.

The attendant came out again and paced down the aisle between the seats. "We are now approaching five thousand feet."

Celeste watched the shadow of their shuttle pass over the white clouds beside them. She spotted another ahead of it, and looked out the window on the left side, to see another shuttleship go past them, heading down to the mainland.

Another minute passed, and they emerged into a greater expanse of blue sky.

"We are nearing our destination at eight thousand feet."

The shuttle started turning to get into position for landing, until Celeste could see the island. Beneath its flat top side, a large mass of solid dirt, roots and even vines tapered down.

The shuttle came low over the isle and slowed to a stop, hovering in place. Then its hatch hissed and opened outward and down to rest on the ground, letting in the sunlight.

"You may now exit in an orderly

fashion," the attendant prompted. "You are now guests of the Floating Land."

Momentous anticipation rose in Celeste as she got up from her seat and followed the other passengers down the ramp. She tried to get a look past their heads at the view beyond.

"Please stay away from the edge of the island," a resonant voice called out from somewhere on the right. Several guides stood around the perimeter, a few paces in from the brink, with their arms spread. Their trim pale-blue uniforms were slashed with silver strips that reflected in the daylight. One was speaking into a crystal that somehow amplified his voice. "Make sure you have a levitation pendant to keep you from falling."

A representative waiting at the end of the downramp lowered a necklace around the head of each tourist in the line as they passed. When it was Celeste's turn, she was given one too. She held it up in her hand and looked at it as she followed the crowd drifting farther inland. On a simple black string hung a white glass marble with blue swirls. It must've been what she saw the one tourist put in the box. They must have to return the necklaces once they reached the mainland again. It was too bad; it would've made a good souvenir.

Celeste lifted her head and took her first good look at the Floating Land. It was a level expanse of lush grass in a roughly circular shape, about fifty yards across, with a wide, resplendent mansion in the middle and a few leafy trees on either side. She wondered if the trees could tell they were aloft in the middle of the sky.

She looked up at the sky – or the upper half of it – basking in the glow. Was she actually closer to the sun? She turned to peer past the edge of the island, down at the fields so far below. The trees and homesteads were nothing but specks, the farmland mere strips of different greens, and the shadows of clouds - as well as some of the lower clouds themselves - were small patches that passed lazily over the ground. She could see so far in all directions, until everything became hazed with blue in the distance. She would've thought she'd find it dizzying - as some of the others clearly did - but instead it was exhilarating.

Celeste turned back to survey the isle. A small puffy cloud floated on the left, at about the same height as the island. The breeze brought it in, and it hovered a few inches from the ground, drifting along over the grass. A little boy ran giggling over to it, and put a hand out over its round top as if to pet it, though his hand would only pass through it.

"If you'll all follow me," the same

announcer prompted, "I will be giving a tour of the grounds, before you go inside." Celeste looked around to see that the last of the other tourists had left the shuttle. She joined them as they gravitated into a straggly group behind the guide, who headed to the northeast.

A cumulus cloud approached from the side, larger than the whole island. It drew closer, enshrouding the west half of the isle, and soon they were completely enveloped in a white haze. Cool moisture surrounded her, omnipresent in the air. Celeste looked around in awe. She lifted a hand, and fine water droplets collected on it. She could hardly believe she was *inside* a cloud. It brought back all her childlike wonder, made her feel more like herself than she had in a long time.

There were mutters from the other tourists as they lost sight of everything that was more than a few feet away.

"There is no cause for concern," the guide reassured. "The cloud is entirely harmless, but it will cause low visibility. Please remain in place until the cloud has passed."

A minute later, the fog began to move off to the right, revealing the sunlit lawn again - now sprinkled with dew. Celeste turned her head to watch the cloud scud off the other side of the island, for the most part intact. It must be so surreal to live in a place that the clouds passed right through.

The guide resumed leading the way to the right of the mansion, until they arrived at a small round pond about twenty feet across. Celeste leaned over to peer in at the bottom, wondering how far down it went. Only a few feet; the island itself wasn't very deep. Somehow she hadn't thought there would be a pocket of water on the sky island. Its clear waters allowed sight of several clusters of raw blueish crystals that peeked out from the sides around the inner circumference. Dappled shade danced across half the surface, cast by a nearby elm. "This pond supplies the mansion with drinking water, without relying solely on the barrels that are brought here on shuttles, as our food is. The crystals lining its interior keep it pristine. It is refilled when it rains."

It hadn't occurred to her that it must rain here too. And it would reach this place sooner than the ground below. But then where would it go? It must drain off the edge of the island...and then it would still be dripping onto the land beneath even after the rain had stopped elsewhere. She wouldn't want to live directly under it, especially since it would be draped in noon shadow every day. But if the rainclouds were at a lower altitude than the island...it would still be sunny with clear blue skies up here, even while it was pouring on the rest of the land. It was so peculiar to envision.

The guide showed them around the back of the mansion, where there was a wide patio of large, flat, square stones, then kept onward around the other side of the house. Just before they rounded the corner, Celeste glanced over her shoulder and noticed the top of a shuttle creeping up into sight from below the island's edge. Strange; Celeste thought they only landed at the front to unload and load passengers. That was the direction they came from, after all.

Once the guide brought them back around to the front again, Celeste studied the place while she and the other people approached its open entrance. It was made of blocks of white stone that shone in the sunlight, topped with a gently sloping roof tiled in midnight-blue slate. The front windows on the ground floor were wide, and the main structure had a one-storey wing on each side. Vines with dark green leaves climbed the corners of the building and also coiled around the columns that stood on either side of the front door to support an overhang. The leaves fluttered as Celeste passed between them and stepped inside.

~ *Chapter 4* ~

Princess Raianna sighed, looking out the mansion's front window at the milling tourists. "Must we keep holding these monthly ticket giveaways? It grows so tiresome doing this same thing over and over."

"It's our best chance of finding the White Princess," the counsellor reminded placidly, coming up beside her with his arms folded.

She turned to him, spreading her hands. "It's been twenty years! Don't you think if my sister was going to visit the island, she would have by now?"

"We've only been hosting the lottery for seven. There are thousands of Celestes in the world. But we *are* narrowing down those left to invite."

"Who's to say she even goes by that name anymore? If she was taken in by someone, they could have named her anything."

"She *was* wearing her necklace when she went missing. We have to hope she didn't lose it. Even if she did, then she's just as likely to be any of the other tourists."

Raianna started pacing over the granite floor of the drawing room, the long skirt of her red dress swishing. "I wish we had a way of knowing more about them first.

Last time, there was a Celeste who was sixty-three years old, and another who was only seven."

"At least it's easy to rule them out on sight." The counsellor resumed peering out the glass. "I only saw a few blonde women step off the shuttles today. It shouldn't take me long to follow up on each of them."

"How can we be sure it's her even if she does come? What if she's already been here and gone and we didn't know it?"

The counsellor gave her a slight smile of fond amusement. "Have a little faith, Princess. We will know. If nothing else, the island itself will recognize her."

He headed out through the archway, and Raianna allowed his words to reassure her. The counsellor was almost like a father to her, when she barely remembered her parents. He'd managed the kingdom while she was a minor, had been her invaluable advisor ever since she'd ascended to the throne at just thirteen. He reminded her to be more optimistic sometimes – but she was the pragmatic one; it had always been in her nature to be skeptical. It had never been her who was meant to rule. Not for the first time, Raianna wished for the day her sister would come and lift the onus of leadership from her.

***

As Celeste and the others entered the mansion, a middle-aged man in slate-blue attire came into the hall from an archway on the right. He stopped before them with his hands clasped behind his back, and smiled. "Welcome, everyone! I am the counsellor to the current ruler of The Island in the Air. I will be guiding you on a tour of the mansion today. Please remain in a group and refrain from touching anything."

He held out an arm and started off through an arch on their left, while Celeste and the tourists trailed behind him in a cluster.

"Here's the sitting room," the counsellor began. The dark floorboards were polished to a soft sheen, and several landscape paintings hung on the papered walls above carved wainscoting. A sculpted wooden settee with red upholstery ran the length of the wall on the right, and there were even a few gold or jade vases on marble pedestals in the corners. Celeste had never seen such elegant furnishings, though they didn't exceed practicality.

A servant came out of a door opposite them and gave them a nod in passing.

The counsellor went on, "The retainers of the royal house also live here in the mansion, in several of the dozen rooms on the second floor. Most are native-born islanders, the sole citizens of the Floating Land, whose families have served as loyal subjects for generations. Some of them take on the duties of guides during these tourist events."

The group lingered and looked around at the decor for a minute, with a few admiring mutters.

"On to the dining room." When they headed out the other archway in the far corner, the counsellor gestured to a parted door in the same wall beside them. "That leads down to the cellar, within the very heart of the island."

Ahead, in a nook formed by a dividing wall, the back door stood open a crack. Its inset window, with the sash lifted an inch to let in a fresh breeze, overlooked the patio. In the north wall, two large windows let in plenty of light onto a long, darkwood dining table lined with chairs.

The counsellor crossed the room and proceeded down another hallway, to an arch on the left. They toured the kitchen – where a few cooks were starting to prepare lunch, and which had an adjoining pantry for storing the provisions brought by the shuttles – and the archive library, through a door at the end of the corridor, where matters of state were discussed.

Then the counsellor led them into a spacious room made entirely of white marble. "And this is the throne room, otherwise known as The Hall of the Rising Sun." The whole eastern wall was covered in ceiling-high windows that looked out on a clear view over the edge of the island. Celeste imagined how the people here would have to watch the sun rise from below them, and it would take several hours before its rays even reached the top side of the island. It must be so otherworldly. In the center of the floor was a raised circular dais. "Royal announcements and coronations are made here, while standing on the dais facing east, in the direction of new beginnings."

They continued into the drawing room, with floors of granite, and then ended up back in the same entry hall they'd started in.

Through the arch to the sitting room, Celeste saw a brunette woman in a stately, dark-red dress. She stood with her back to Celeste amidst a gaggle of curious tourists.

"Thank you all for coming!" the counsellor concluded to the group Celeste was in. "You may resume exploring the island. A shuttle should be arriving shortly with another load of tourists from the mainland. You can take it back down once they disembark."

Most of the people started filtering out the open front door. But Celeste lingered, a little disappointed as she looked around. She didn't want to leave already. After so many years of wishing, it didn't seem sufficient to just visit the island for barely an hour. Besides, her ticket was for a 'day trip'. Maybe she could just take a later shuttle back.

The counsellor came up to her. "Good day. Are you by chance the recipient of one of the golden tickets for a free trip?"

"Oh - yes," she replied, fishing the ticket out of her pocket to show him.

He leaned a bit closer to inspect the name on it. "Then you're eligible for an exclusive tour of the royal portrait gallery!" He turned aside and gestured with a hand.

Celeste was delighted. It was just the kind of thing she'd been hoping for. Maybe it was a little overgenerous, when she'd already gotten a free pass here in the first place, but she wasn't about to turn down the chance to stay longer and see a special room.

The counsellor went to open a door up the hall on the right, and they entered a long, narrow gallery with gold-inlaid floors. Dozens of large paintings in gilded frames hung side-by-side along the length of the left-hand wall. "The Silverborn family has ruled this island for as long as it has been in the sky," the counsellor began as they paced down the row of portraits of past kings and queens.

Near the end, they stopped in front of one depicting a regal couple sitting together. The brunette woman held a blonde baby girl in a white dress, perched on her knee. The man had fair hair sweeping halfway to his shoulders, and a beard only around his mouth. There was a gentle wisdom in his eyes.

"These were the last rulers of the Floating Land," the counsellor said with a trace of sadness in his voice. "They both perished of fever when their second daughter was only seven years old. It was a great loss for us all."

"Is that her?" Celeste prompted, indicating the baby in the picture.

"No, this is their firstborn, the White Princess."

Celeste paused, studying the girl's green eyes. They looked somehow familiar.

"She was always destined to be the one true ruler of the Floating Land, for she possessed the wise and just nature needed in a Preserver of Peace. But, nineteen years ago, she went missing from the island, when she was little more than a year old."

Celeste looked at the counsellor in commiserative dismay.

"We searched the whole mansion and grounds, and began to worry that she'd fallen off. She did wear her levitation pendant at all times, so she'd be safe, but she could still be suspended in the air anywhere around or below the island.

"Then we noticed several of our expensive items were gone as well. A shuttle had recently departed after delivering a shipment of supplies, and we realized the only ones who could have done it were the delivery men." As an aside, the counsellor added, "Back then, it wasn't uncommon for the freighter to be our only visitor in the whole month. After that, we had the unloaders just leave the crates on the lawn, and only let our own trusted retainers bring them inside the mansion." Then he turned back to regard the portrait. "We feared the thieves had taken the Princess too, and planned to hold her for ransom. We sent out shuttles in every direction to try to catch them, but by then they were long gone. They hadn't landed the shuttle on the mainland anywhere near here, so they must have driven it back to their hideout. We scoured the land for miles around, asking everyone if they'd seen a blonde tot matching the White Princess' description, or any suspicious sellers of stolen merchandise, for that matter.

"Time went on, but a ransom demand never came. We wondered if perhaps the Princess had accidentally stowed away on board their shuttle and they didn't know it. If that was the case, we hoped they'd let her go once they discovered her. But we found no trace of her in the area. We persisted for weeks, but we only have so many people that could be sent out, and our jurisdiction only extends so far. We couldn't cover the whole world. So, dejected, we returned to our island, knowing she must be in one of the distant places we hadn't gotten to yet."

Celeste had listened enrapt to it all. She'd never heard word of this back in the southwest.

"Without her, the island is slowly deteriorating, which it never has before. We used to be at a height of ten thousand feet. Now it is sinking lower by a hundred feet each year."

Celeste's heart lurched. *Oh no.*

"The island was once larger as well, but its edges have been crumbling, a little every week. In less than eighty years, the Floating Land will be nothing more than a pile of earth on the ground - if there's anything left of it at all."

She put a hand over her chest. It would be a tragedy if such a marvel of nature were to be no more.

"But we retain the hope that the White Princess will return one day to take her rightful place on the throne, and restore our land to its proper balance." The counsellor looked right at her. "Her name is Celeste."

Her stomach leapt. "That's my name," she murmured.

He showed a rueful smile. "I know. In each batch of those free tickets we've been sending out, twenty of them are addressed to women named Celeste, in the hopes that one of them turns out to be our Princess."

"Oh." Celeste felt easier about it, if a little sheepish. Of course she wasn't the only one.

They moved on to the next painting. "And this one is Raianna, the red princess." It was an elegant young woman in a crimson dress, standing proud with her hands folded at her waist and her chin up. Her brunette hair cascaded down her shoulders, but there was something about her stern brown eyes and hard cheekbones that made her seem older than she must have been. "You may have seen her around the mansion. Only a year younger than Celeste, she's been the reigning princess since she was thirteen. She never knew her sister, but she's been waiting for her for nineteen years."

~ Chapter 5 ~

Celeste and the counsellor came out of the gallery into the back room of the mansion. They stood for a moment in somber silence as Celeste thought about the stories of the Silverborns. Then she lifted her head, catching the faintest whiff.

"Does something on the air smell odd to you?" she asked the counsellor in a murmur, drifting to the slightly ajar back door to investigate. When she stopped just back from it, a whisper of wind came through the gap under the partially lifted window-pane. There was definitely a cold metallic scent on the breeze, with an almost sickly element to it that seemed much more sinister.

On the patio ahead, there were two fellows tinkering with a large steel canister. Celeste had a very unsafe feeling. She closed and locked the door, just for caution's sake. Beyond the men, a shuttle with an open hatch waited near the edge of the island. Then she saw a vague shimmering in the air to the right, a wavering zigzag line almost of cloud, but it was gone again in a trice. She slid the window down for good measure, ensuring it was shut tight. Whatever it was, it was clearly airborne.

The men noticed it, too, and appeared to be spurred into fear by it; when the shuttle veered and made a getaway, they came rushing up to the door and tried to get inside, but the handle wouldn't move.

"Let us in!" they shouted desperately through the glass, banging on it with their fists. "There's some kind of vapour out here..." They glanced over their shoulders apprehensively, where increasing amounts of wisps now floated. Celeste didn't want to leave them out there to be victimized, but she didn't want to risk letting the smokelike substance in with them, either.

Then, seeing that the men were backed into a corner, the mist struck, insinuating itself under their nostrils so it was drawn in with their next breath. A change seemed to come over them, and before her eyes they turned into ravening beasts, their human features distorted into vulturous parody with sharp pink skin and clawlike hands.

"No..." Celeste breathed in horror, backing away.

"Open the door..." the one on the left, in a red captain's coat, snarled teasingly in an entirely different voice. He pulled out the pistol that hung at his belt, pointing it straight at her from behind the glass, the hard muzzle pressed right up against it.

Alarmed, Celeste cast around for a place to take cover; she doubted that even the thick double panes would stop a bullet from passing through. Then, through the archway behind her, she saw a swarm of the infected monsters beginning to pour in from the front of the house.

She stared with a sinking dread in her middle. She hadn't locked the front door.

She turned back to the deeper half of the room, and to her shock found that even the counsellor hadn't been spared; the contagion must already be spreading on the air the others had let in.

With no choice left to her, she whirled

and fled down the stairs into the dark earthen cellar, hoping at least to escape their notice by hiding there, until she could think of some other way out.

Once she reached the bottom landing she slowed, looking around cautiously. The walls and ceiling were overgrown with gnarly roots and even thick green vines, hanging down like verdant stalactites. Beyond the dim circle of light from the mounted candle behind her, the shadowy basement faded into near blackness; she couldn't tell how long it went on for, but it seemed quiet and spacious.

In the hopes of finding a tunnel that led away from there, Celeste ventured deeper. She bent lower to clear the overhead curtain of branchlike growths, and wove between individual dangling stems.

She brushed against the leaves of a trailing ivy, and suddenly there was a soft white glow in the air around her, lighting the way. The draped roots lifted, parting to either side to show her a clear path ahead through the tangle. The plants nearby rustled though there were no drafts, almost as if whispering, "Princess...princess."

Celeste looked down at herself, and realized that the radiance was coming from her own dress, which was now a pristine white. Lifting her head, she regarded a drooping vine beside her, and raised her hand under it. It curled around to set itself gently on her palm, responding to her wordless beckon. And then she understood.

She was the White Princess.

And she knew what she had to do.

Turning back the way she had come, she hastened for the staircase through a lane of provided airspace that closed again behind her, as the shine of her gown gradually receded. As she went up the steps, a contingent of vines followed her through the air alongside, reaching and growing at the same speed as her travel.

At the top floor, Celeste sent her vines forward to touch the few affected individuals that had roamed into the vicinity. Upon contact, the leaves conveyed their healing, ridding them of the wisps' possession and returning the people to their original selves. Some of them buckled where they stood, as if drained of energy from the frenzy, or made unconscious by events they would rather forget.

***

The red princess shook her head to clear away the shadow darkening her vision. As awareness returned to her, she realized she was on her hands and knees. The last thing she remembered was being attacked by vulture-like creatures... She must have turned into one too. She lifted her head to look out the sitting room archway. What she saw was a blonde woman in a pure white gown, standing at the center of a mass of vines. They darted out in the direction of her every glance and gesture, wrapping themselves around each creature that came at her, restoring them to their human forms.

She can control the vines, Raianna thought, with dawning awe.

...Sister...

***

A crash sounded behind Celeste, and she glanced over her shoulder. Outside the back door, the creature in the red coat was striking his pistol against the window, fracturing the glass and dislodging shattered fragments. He'd already broken through the first pane. Once he'd made a hole big enough in the second, he reached his arm through and unlocked the door. As soon as he shoved it open, Celeste had her vines lash forth to meet him and his associate. The two stopped short in their charge, and their faces regained their identity. The man on the right slumped to the floor, out cold, but the captain only sagged, leaning hands on his knees.

Celeste redirected her attention to the last few of the afflicted who were still trying to get at her, and treated them too. Then she surveyed the room, but saw no more vulturous beasts. Several of the people were coming to, clambering to their feet with faint groans and sighs. Celeste let the vines withdraw back into the cellar.

She heard the click of a cocking gun.

She turned abruptly, but the captain had already aimed his pistol. The bullet he fired instantly pierced her near the heart, biting her with a sharp pang. She collapsed onto her back, and lay there in staring shock for a moment. She had never expected he would still wish her harm after he'd been cured. He leapt over her on his way past. Her eyelids grew heavy, and she could feel the darkness creeping in on her, the pain sapping her strength. Before long, her head lolled to the side, and the life went out of her.

***

The crack of a gunshot made Raianna whip around. Her stomach dropped with dread. She pushed her way through the interposing crowd, through the archway to the back room.

And there she came upon the body of her dead sister, shot through the chest, a spread of blood staining her pristine white gown. That was the one place the colour red should never appear. Grimly Raianna turned to see the man with the smoking gun flee out the front entrance, pursued by a mob of outraged subjects. The princess in crimson stormed out after him, eyes blazing.

He ran to the very edge of the jutting grass-covered cliff, then turned back to the horde, which had stopped some distance back from the precipice. He pointed his pistol at them. He seemed to think that his escape was assured, as a shuttlecraft sluggishly rose through the clouds from below.

But then the ground under his feet gave way, the tip of the crag crumbling down toward a sheer miles-long drop, and he lost hold of his gun even as the red princess continued striding out from the throng toward him. At her command, the vines and roots in the remaining cliffside whipped out to catch him, lifting him up before her so she could stare at him face to face when she stopped just inches away – but then the bonds started tightening, coiling ever more constrictively around his limbs, his body...his neck.

From the crowd behind, the counsellor stepped closer to her. "Don't do it," he pleaded softly. But Raianna's gaze on the captain was merciless. He was going to pay for what he had done to her precious sister, so newly found, so senselessly lost.

***

The blood of the princess in white seeped through the ground of her home, down to the very heart of the Floating Land. There, the living consciousness recognized its beloved queen, recalled its primary instinct to protect her. The healing of the vines was redirected back through the earth to where Celeste lay crumpled, giving back what she had expended to the others of her people, but had not partaken of herself. Her gown began to glow again, clearing away the bloodstains, before fading.

Slowly, her eyes opened again to reveal pearl-grey irises, which reverted to their original green as she took a breath that set her heart to beating. Blinking, Celeste carefully stood up, and turned to survey the scene out the open front door. By the clifftop, her sister looked over her shoulder, and her vines' grip on the captain slackened as she saw with wonder that Celeste was alive.

The White Princess headed out to them, her steps measured and sure. The crowd parted for her, watching her with murmurs of amazement.

"...the Princess..."

"She lives!"

Celeste arrived beside her sister, gaze on the captain. "Set him down," she said calmly. "He knows not what he did."

Still staring at Celeste, Raianna had the vines unwind from around the captain's neck, then brought him back in so his feet touched the ground - but the roots stayed securely wrapped around his arms, to make sure he didn't try anything.

The man was panting through his ragged throat, his eyes wide on Celeste. "You...I shot you..." he whispered hoarsely.

Celeste looked the captain square in the eye. "Take him and his accomplice to a correctional facility. Make sure they do enough selfless service to make up for what they've done."

"Yes, Princess," the counsellor agreed. He sent some men to gather the other criminal, and had a guard clamp cuffs on the captain's hands, so Raianna could withdraw the vines. Then the offenders were marched onto the very shuttle they'd been planning to commandeer as an escape.

The red princess turned to Celeste, extending both hands toward hers. "Sister," she breathed, and Celeste smiled at her, holding her hands and giving them a squeeze.

"Sorry I've been away so long. I never knew about any of this."

"I'm just grateful you're safe. But now that you're here, the people will wonder..." Raianna murmured, looking around at the crowd.

"I know." Celeste's eyes were lowered. "I'll make the announcement. Have them gather in the throne room." It needed to be done - even though it meant she'd have to leave her foster mother behind. At least Farmer Ramsey would be satisfied that she'd found a home of her own. Maybe Celeste could even send some royal funds their way. After things were settled here, she would go back to the mainland to explain the situation to her family. She hoped they'd understand. Her people needed her here, to keep the island from falling apart.

As Raianna herded all the inhabitants of the island into the mansion, Celeste folded her hands, pensive gaze still on the ground. It all made sense - the story of how the White Princess had disappeared along with a long-distance shuttle, and her own history of how the Ramseys had found her abandoned in a remote field far in the southwest. The royal couple in the portrait had been her parents. She was sad she'd never known them, that she wouldn't get a chance to, now – sad that they were gone altogether. They looked like they had been good-hearted people.

The counsellor came back up to her from the island edge. "It's good to have you back, Princess," he said softly.

She met his eyes. "You knew my parents, before. Will you tell me more about them?"

He smiled. "I'd be honoured to." He set a hand on her shoulder as he headed past.

Drawing in a deep breath of crisp air, Celeste looked around at the island, and smiled. She didn't only consider it her duty to stay here. She loved this place. It was where she belonged.

Turning, Celeste proceeded inside, head up and shoulders squared. She entered the Hall of the Rising Sun, where the few dozen native islanders and attendants of the royal family stood in a semicircle, watching Celeste with expectant hope. Raianna and the counsellor were foremost among them.

Pristine gown draping sedately on the floor behind her, Celeste stepped up onto the large circular marble dais, facing east with stature proud. "I am Celeste Silverborn, the White Princess and one true ruler of the Island in the Air. I have returned to my home, and protected it once already from the threat of harm. I have been brought back to life, to take my place as Preserver of Peace!" And the citizens cheered.

The End

www.ingramcontent.com/pod-product-compliance
Lightning Source LLC
Chambersburg PA
CBHW071157100726
47908CB00002B/411
* 9 7 8 1 7 7 5 0 2 5 2 7 6 *